STARGAZER

THE LAND OF ELYON BOOK 4

STARGAZER

PATRICK CARMAN

SCHOLASTIC INC.

New York Toronto London Auckland
Sydney Mexico City New Delhi Hong Kong

ISBN-13: 978-0-545-21276-2
ISBN-10: 0-545-21276-6

12 11 10 9 8 7 6 5 4 3 2 1   9 10 11 12 13 14/0

Printed in the U.S.A.   40

First Scholastic paperback printing, November 2009

For my mom and dad

Who took separate paths and still managed to show me the way home

THE LAND OF ELYON

THE FIVE STONE PI

LLARS

INTRODUCTION

Stargazer is the fifth Land of Elyon book. If you're new to the series or feel you might have forgotten some of what has taken place so far, the following brief descriptions of each book might prove useful. Enjoy!

The Land of Elyon story begins with *The Dark Hills Divide*, in which a curious young girl named Alexa Daley refuses to stay trapped behind the walls that surround her small town. Through persistence (and sneakiness), Alexa discovers a hidden passageway into the wild world outside, where animals have their own ideas about the walls that dominate the landscape. With a little help from Murphy—an energetic squirrel of the woods—and a surprisingly tiny forest dweller named Yipes, Alexa begins to unravel the mysteries that lay hidden all around her.

In *Beyond the Valley of Thorns*, the second Elyon book, Alexa's journey becomes more perilous. She leaves the safety of her home and travels across the Land of Elyon. Along the way she befriends the giant Armon, fights the evil forces of Victor Grindall, and goes to battle against an army of ogres. Some of the biggest secrets in the Land of Elyon are revealed in *Beyond the Valley of Thorns*, but the biggest secret of them all is still hidden from Alexa's view.

The Tenth City, the final book in the core Elyon trilogy, brings all the forces of good and evil against one another. Alexa discovers her true identity as she fights alongside Murphy, Yipes, and Armon. Evil has left the shores of Alexa's home when *The Tenth City* comes to an end, but it searches for a new place to corrupt.

The prequel to the Elyon trilogy, *Into the Mist*, has been called both a prequel *and* a continuation of the story. Both are true. *Into the Mist* is told from the deck of the *Warwick Beacon* after Yipes and Alexa have left the Land of Elyon in search of new adventures. The *Warwick Beacon* is captained by Roland Warvold, brother of Thomas Warvold, the architect of the walls that appear in *The Dark Hills Divide*. Roland tells Alexa and Yipes the story of his own childhood with his brother Thomas, and we see them at their most magical—escaping from a vile orphanage, overcoming the Wakefield House, and meeting Armon for the first time. When *Into the Mist* comes to an end, Roland has finished his story and the *Warwick Beacon* has arrived at the Five Stone Pillars.

The Five Stone Pillars are a hidden realm Alexa and Yipes know nothing about. The evil Abaddon, in the form of a sea monster, has followed them and wants to rule the Five Stone Pillars. He will stop at nothing to gain control of the place and its people.

As we begin *Stargazer* together, Alexa's journey has taken her far from home, across the Lonely Sea, to a place where she will at last discover her true purpose. . . .

PART I

Into the Realm of
Lost Children

CHAPTER I

THE VOICE OF
THE ENEMY

A long voyage includes days without wind or waves.
The boat sits still on deep water, waiting for a push. The
morning sun shines through the surface of the Lonely Sea
into unknown depths of blue water, and I often leaned
over the side of the *Warwick Beacon* in search of the
murky outline of a fish. A shadow the size and shape of
my forearm would drift past my line of sight and disappear under the boat. Then I would race to the other side
and look down, waiting until the shadow re-emerged and
slowly disappeared out into the sea. On a calm day, it was
not uncommon for me to spend an hour or more at this
entirely useless undertaking.

But this morning, as I leaned out over the edge of the
rail, my heart caught in my throat at the thought of what
I might see.

To begin with, we'd found the Five Stone Pillars, a
mysterious place hidden far away from The Land of
Elyon. We could see the pillars clearly, less than a nauti-
cal mile away, rising out of the sea. From all I'd been told,
I knew this was an especially secret place, where Sir
Alistair Wakefield hid the lost children so that no danger
could find them.

But danger *had* found the lost children. And what's worse, we were the ones who'd brought the danger to them. Something had been following our ship since the very beginning of our long journey away from The Land of Elyon. It was something unseen and sinister, watching our every move from the depths of the sea.

I'd been standing at the rail for a while, looking into the calmest water I'd ever seen, wishing that the wind would kick up and send us on our way. There was a terrible chill in the air as I scanned the glassy surface, hoping not to spot anything larger than my own boot.

"Captain?" asked Yipes, my tiny, ever-present companion. "Why is everything so still?" I chanced a fleeting look away from the smooth surface of the water and saw that he was standing very near our captain, Roland Warvold, questioning him.

Yipes tapped Roland in the leg with his finger. "Pardon me, sir."

The captain didn't respond. We had come within sight of our long-awaited destination, but it felt as if we were anchored in place, and Roland was busy reviewing his charts and maps at the wheel of the boat. Yipes is the sort of person who has a hard time being ignored, so he kept at it, tap tap tapping at the knee in front of his face until finally Roland could stand it no more.

"Can't you find something useful to do?" Roland replied. He knelt down so that he was at eye level with

Yipes, and the two began to talk as I returned to watching the Lonely Sea.

The water was so smooth and still I couldn't stand looking at it any longer without dropping something in and breaking the glass surface. I swung around, searching the deck for something to throw, and my eyes lit on the remains of a breakfast that had yet to be cleaned up. It was only a few steps away, and when I arrived there I found several things to choose from that would suit my purpose. I picked up a string of fish bones by its crispy tail and walked back toward the rail of the boat.

"You see there," said Roland. "At least Alexa is trying to make herself useful."

Yipes protested, citing the fact that he'd *made* the breakfast and didn't think it was fair that he should have to clean up. I tossed the fish bones into the water and watched as the ripples circled out and bumped lazily into the side of the boat. The bones were light enough to float, which was unfortunate, because they were an ugly addition to what had been a rather enjoyable (if boring) view of things. I began to think about how I might fish the leftover breakfast out of the water, and as I did, there came a thin shadow up from the depths of the sea. It looked as if it was about the size of the very fish I'd thrown overboard, and I was curious about what sort of small sea creature it was.

The shadow grew darker as it neared the surface. Suddenly alert, I looked more carefully and saw that this was no ordinary shadow — it was long and it grew wider from the tip down. The water behind the fish bones began to move ever so slightly. Big, rolling movement that was almost imperceptible, as if something huge was moving many feet below.

I heard a soft, crackling sound and watched as the shadow emerged from the water. It had the look of weather-beaten metal, like a sword or a shield after being in salty water for a hundred years. Clustered along its length were barnacles and jagged crustaceans. It looked like an ancient, metal snake for a split second when it rose from the water, but that rapidly changed. It unfurled itself and spread out thin and low over the bones on the water. Unrolled, this thing was as wide as the wheel of the ship, full of a strange energy. Ghostly sparks sizzled against the wide, flat inside. It stopped a moment and seemed to look at me, then slowly enveloped all the space around the bones, the water boiling as it came near. As I gasped, it curled back into the rolled-up shape it had been, the bones in its clutches, and became a shadow under the water. The water rippled, the shadow disappeared, and all was still once more.

It seemed to me that the whole incident occurred outside of time. It had seemed slow and yet the whole event was over before I could think to cry out to Roland and Yipes about what was happening.

I waited another moment at the rail, waiting to see if the shadow would return, but it did not.

"Roland!" I yelled across the boat. He and Yipes approached and I pointed to where the bones had been.

"Something came out of the water," I said. "It seemed small at first, like a tentacle. But then it unwound like a blanket. I think whatever it was is attached to something bigger."

"How much bigger?" asked Yipes. His eyes were round and white with concern. When I didn't answer, he darted to the breakfast table and returned with another row of fish bones.

"Maybe that's not such a good idea," said Roland. Yipes had his arm back with the fish bones by the tail, about to hurl them into the water. "Whatever's out there, we don't want it thinking it can find a lot of food near the boat."

This seemed to strike Yipes as a very good thought, and he dropped the bones on the deck, then wiped his hand on Roland's leg.

Roland looked down at me and placed a hand on my shoulder.

"Are you sure of what you saw?" he asked. "We've been out here for almost thirty days. The sea can play tricks on you after a while."

"I'm sure," I said, a little wounded that Roland wasn't certain he could believe me. "It looked like it was made of old armor or metal on the outside, but on the inside —

when it unrolled — it was like nothing I've ever seen. It sparked with blue and yellow lines, like it was bursting with energy."

"*Electricity,*" mumbled Roland.

"What was that you said?" asked Yipes. Neither he nor I had ever heard the word used before.

"It's nothing," answered Roland, but I could tell that it was important. "Just something Sir Alistair Wakefield was experimenting with. I only knew of it in passing."

I began to question him, but the captain would have none of it.

"We have to be ready for what might come next," he said.

Yipes was alarmed by this comment and jumped onto the rail, where he could almost look Roland in the eye.

"*What* might come next?" Yipes asked, fidgeting nervously with one long side of his mustache.

"Who can say?"

Yipes was beside himself, which was common in situations like this. "Just a moment ago, you said something might come next. What did you mean?"

"Alexa, you and Yipes go below and bring the harpoons," said Roland. "The ones with the shortest ropes."

Yipes wasn't getting the answer he was looking for, and he began grasping at straws.

"There must be some way you could make the wind blow, maybe a spell or a potion you've found in your travels," he said. Roland and I looked at him like he'd gone crazy.

"We can't just sit here and wait for *what might come next*, whatever that is!"

Roland drew his line of sight toward the Five Stone Pillars and saw that they were still a ways off.

"The wind will blow when it wants to, not a moment sooner," he said. "We'll need to be on our guard until then."

And so it was that we each took up a different position on the *Warwick Beacon* and watched the still water all around us, waiting for something awful to rise from the sea. Yipes and I both carried small knives we used for preparing food or cutting a rope, and Roland had what Yipes and I liked to call the *real* sword, but other than that, the harpoons were the only seaworthy weapons we had. The harpoons were long but not very heavy, with sharp points and a length of rope attached to their ends. The sharp points were followed down the shaft by metal barbs meant to dig in and hold tight. I wasn't sure I wanted to hold on to whatever was in the water if it showed itself again.

Morning made its maddeningly slow march to afternoon, afternoon lurched into early evening, and then came dusk. All the while we waited in silence for a wind that was busy somewhere else in the world and a monster that would not show its face. Over and over

9

again, I whispered to myself, *Please send the wind, Elyon. Please, send the wind.*

When dusk turned to night, Yipes went below and made a hasty dinner of piping hot tea and biscuits he'd cooked up the day before. We huddled together at the wheel of the boat with steaming cups and tried to make the best of things.

"There's really nothing quite so nice as a spot of tea and a biscuit, don't you think?" Yipes asked. He took a big bite of his dinner and chased it with a sip from the cup. For a man of such tiny proportions, Yipes had quite an appetite. He tipped his floppy hat, smiling as he chewed. His mustache, long in need of a trim, wobbled as he chewed. And those bright eyes of his crinkled at the corners and burst with energy.

"We'll be getting tired soon," said Roland. "I'll take the first watch while you two get some sleep. I expect we'll be moving again by morning."

"How do you know when the wind will return?" I asked.

Roland sipped his tea and fiddled with the wheel of the boat. The color had long been washed out of his clothing, and his white shirt stood in stark contrast to his darkly tanned face. A daily onslaught of wind and sun had done things to his hair and beard and face that made them magical to look at.

"After ten thousand nights at sea," he said, "a sailor knows a thing or two about the ways of the wind."

We whispered a while longer and then Roland got up

and walked to the front of the *Warwick Beacon*. When I looked at Yipes, he was already lying back, counting the display of stars in the night sky. I had known him long enough to feel certain that he would only lie awake for a short time before sleep would take him.

"I wonder what's at the top of the five pillars," he mumbled, but his eyes were already turning heavy and dull.

"Candies and treats," I said. "And tea. *Lots* of tea."

Yipes breathed in deep and let out a nice long *mmm-mmmm*. Then I was sure he was asleep and dreaming. It would prove harder for me to find rest, but after a while I, too, was asleep on the deck. I know this only because of my eventual awakening to an unexpected feeling of warmth. When I opened my eyes, I saw that there was indeed a blanket very near my face, hovering a few feet in the air and surrounding my entire body. The crackling sound of — what was it called? — *electricity* sparked in the air above me. Though it had no eyes that I could see, the shape of the energy itself moved with yellows and blues over the surface and created the appearance of a murky face. It felt as if it might be looking at me from somewhere in the unseen depths of the water below. And then I heard a familiar voice meant only for me.

You didn't think I would be defeated so easily did you, Alexa Daley?

It was the dreadful sound of the darkest force in the world.

Abaddon.

11

I tried to move to one side, but the darkness glided over with me. And what was worse, it moved lower still, the shadowy face closer and growing hotter.

It pleases me to see you there, afraid of what comes next, wishing you could escape me.

"But you were destroyed," I said, a shaking whisper all I could manage. "Elyon did away with you."

Oh, no, not destroyed, only different.

The words were followed by a hissing laughter. The water began to move under the *Warwick Beacon*.

It's not as enjoyable to be trapped underwater as you might think. I prefer dry land. How convenient that you've led me to it!

"Yipes!" I cried. "Get up! Get up!"

Yipes was an unusually deep sleeper and it took something loud and close in order to wake him. The danger in waking Yipes with a start at times of peril is that he springs into action before he's fully awake.

"What is it? What?" Yipes was up in a flash, bouncing back and forth on the deck, wielding his little wooden handled bread knife as though it were a spear. Roland had also come running from the front of the ship, where he'd been looking out at the still water. I realized something then that I hadn't before: Only I could hear the voice of Abaddon. Until I'd yelled out for Yipes, it had been quiet on the boat.

Roland had his sword unsheathed and was soon standing by my side.

12

"Stay still, Alexa!" he yelled. The sizzling blanket of Abaddon curled back into a cylinder and began sliding on its long arm across the rail. Roland was holding his sword low near the deck. As I rolled out of the way, he sliced upward, ripping into scales of metal and stone clusters collected from the deep. Roland fell back, stunned by some force he hadn't expected, and there came a shrieking sound from somewhere far below us. He had not severed the piece, but it was clear that he had angered whatever was at the other end. The curled snake rose high in the air over the *Warwick Beacon*, its encrusted metal scales clanking as it went. It seemed to gather energy from the inside, the metal scales turning orange before our eyes. And then, with a sudden burst, the whole length was on fire, slapping the surface of the *Warwick Beacon* like a flaming whip. Everywhere it pounded, it left burning patches along the top of the deck.

"Try the harpoons!" Roland cried. He had recovered from whatever force had taken his breath away and was standing again. Yipes was already climbing as only Yipes could. He was quickly near the top of the highest mast with the rope to his harpoon between his teeth. When he arrived where he could look down on the flaming beast, he wrapped his legs around the mast and hauled the harpoon up into his hand by the rope. He waited only a moment, then threw with all his might.

And what a shot it was! The harpoon hit something soft right between the metal scales of the monster and

13

slid through to the other side. The shrieking sound from beneath the *Warwick Beacon* returned, and this time the snake of flaming steel retreated for its watery home. The Lonely Sea boiled and smoked, and I heard Yipes howling from high above as the rope burned through his fingers and shot out into the open water, trailing behind the wicked arm of Abaddon.

Roland pointed toward two smoldering fires on the deck of the ship. "We must put those out!" he called.

This command sent us all swiftly into action. Yipes slid down the mast and pounded the nearest flame with his boots while Roland and I stamped out the larger of the two. There came a moment then when everything was very quiet as we listened for the sound of evil lurking near in the waters. I could already see the very beginning of a new day far off on the horizon. We'd slept a lot longer than I realized, and very soon it would be morning. Abaddon had come in the deepest part of the night for one purpose: to tell me that I'd not only failed to destroy him, but that I'd shown him the way to an innocent place he could ruin. A place he could call home.

"Do you feel that?" I asked.

"Feel what?" asked Yipes, troubled by the thought of what I might have noticed. But he needn't have been afraid, for Roland had been right about what the morning would bring.

The salty sea wind had returned.

14

CHAPTER 2

DOWN WITH
THE SHIP

In all my experience with my dear friends Yipes and Roland, I never imagined they could move so fast and with such purpose. As the sun began to rise on the distant horizon, they jumped and dashed to every high and low part of the ship, setting the sails free on the wind with alarming speed and accuracy. No rope tangled, no knot was left untied, and each of the giant sails stretched tight with wind as sunlight burst onto the water from the east.

"We're moving!" shouted Yipes from where he dangled high at the top of the main mast.

"Stay up and keep watch on the water!" yelled Roland. "I want to know if we're being followed."

"It will be my pleasure, Captain!"

Yipes liked to hang from high, unsafe places and look down on the rest of the world. I used to worry about this all the time, but then I grew used to the idea that he was at his best in situations like these.

"Alexa," cried Roland from the wheel. "To the bow! Watch for obstacles in our path."

Roland wanted me at the front of the boat, but I couldn't imagine what he'd meant by *obstacles*. We were hundreds of miles out to sea — what obstacles could there be? When I arrived at the bow, I leaned out, watching the windswept surface of the water for anything unusual. I kept glancing over my shoulder, expecting to see something rise from the water and demolish us from behind, but Yipes remained silent from atop the mast and we maintained our course toward the Five Stone Pillars.

When we'd cut the distance we needed to travel almost in half, Roland turned the *Warwick Beacon* sharply to the right and I pitched sideways along a rail made slick from decades of wear on the Lonely Sea.

"Hold on!" he yelled. There was a crushing thud as the ship lurched at the impact of an unyielding mass beneath the surface. Before I could fully recover my balance, Roland launched the boat in another direction and I slid back toward the middle, staring into the blue sky. High above on the mast, Yipes was perfectly still, holding on as Roland had told us to do. He had turned his gaze to the front of the *Warwick Beacon*.

"What's happening?" I called to Roland.

"The Five Stone Pillars aren't the only rock formations in the Lonely Sea," he replied. "We've entered the Crossing of the Narrows and our approach will be complicated from this direction."

"Farther to the right!" howled Yipes. "Farther to the right!"

Roland spun the wheel free and fast, and I stood, working my way along the rail.

"Isn't there another way?" I asked.

"There is, but it's the long way around. I don't think we want to be on the water any longer than we have to be."

There was no doubt about the need to get free of the Lonely Sea by the fastest way imaginable, even if it meant crossing through a death-defying labyrinth. I wanted to ask what the Crossing of the Narrows was, but I was cut short by another cry from above.

"Now the left! The left!"

No one was watching the back of the *Warwick Beacon*, and I had a terrible feeling about what could be taking us by surprise. As Roland and Yipes navigated a sea strewn with the shadows of rising stone, I struggled to reach the tail of the boat. The hull was slammed hard once more and I lost my grip, tumbling end over end.

"Straighten up, Roland! Right up the middle now!" Yipes instructed. "There's only a foot to spare on either side!"

I grabbed for the railing and looked toward the Five Stone Pillars. We were close, and I realized with dread that there was no obvious way to the top. There was only jagged rock shooting up into the sky, ending in wide plateaus. I made the final dash to the back of the *Warwick Beacon* and held tight as the ship bounced hard, nearly throwing me into the depths of the sea. And then I saw Abaddon for what he had truly become: A vast black shadow within the Lonely Sea was carefully approaching. Watching it overtake the *Warwick Beacon* reminded me of a blue sky turning

17

suddenly dark with thick rain clouds. And it made me feel the same way, as if a great storm was about to pound our wooden boat into oblivion. The shadow drifted under the boat and I realized the dreadful truth: The sea monster Abaddon was bigger by far than the boat we sailed on.

"Faster!" I screamed. "The monster is moving underneath us!"

Glancing up quickly, I saw that Yipes had seen it, too, and he was terrified of what was happening. The Crossing of the Narrows had grown impossible to navigate without the hull meeting stone barriers at every turn, and the shadow of the sea monster had come fully around us.

"Charge for the pillars!" cried Yipes. "There's no other way!"

Roland kept the ship straight, crashing the hull over and over as we came directly up to the first of the Five Stone Pillars. The *Warwick Beacon* was taking on water. We were sinking into the Lonely Sea, and what was worse, Abaddon had begun to show himself once more. Looking over the back of the ship, I saw the horrible head of the monster rise out of the water. It was round and covered in rusted metal and it rolled open with the sound of chains to reveal a row of sparking metallic teeth.

Time to go down with the ship, Alexa. You've served your purpose!

The head rolled shut and disappeared into the depths of the sea. It was replaced by not one but dozens of gruesome metal arms moving up out of the water on every side of our ship. Like ancient prison bars surfaced with iron scales and barnacles, they surrounded us, dangling in the air with electricity sparking blue and yellow between them.

"Hold on!" yelled Roland. "Hold on!"

I held the handrail with an iron grip and we sailed headlong into the base of the pillar before us. The *Warwick Beacon* splintered apart at the bow and began filling with water from the shattered hull. Roland let go of the wheel and took a harpoon in hand, and I watched in horror as the metal arms of Abaddon turned orange and red, then exploded into flames.

"Come get them!" screamed Roland. "Come and take them now!"

What was he saying? It was as if he were screaming for Abaddon to devour both Yipes and me, and for an instant I doubted my old friend and protector. The arms of Abaddon batted the *Warwick Beacon* from every side with flaming whips, and the ship tipped hard and fast up at the tail, its shattered head submerging into the Lonely Sea.

"Come and get them *NOWWWW!*" howled Roland. He threw his harpoon and it cut through scales of fire, the barbs holding firm to a writhing arm of the beast. I was spellbound by the sheer madness of the chaos at sea, unable to do anything but rise on the tail end of a sinking ship and watch as the captain took hold of the wheel once more. He looked back at me, my beloved uncle Roland, and said his last words.

19

"Look to the sky, Alexa Daley! It is there your future lies!"

The flaming metal arms of Abaddon took hold of the *Warwick Beacon* from every side and pulled downward. I held the rail where I stood at the back of the ship, my legs dangling free as the ship's tail tipped high into the air. Roland tumbled over the wheel and into the water, where an arm of metal scales and flames pulled him under.

"No!" I cried. "Give him back! Give him back!"

The captain was gone, Yipes was nowhere to be seen, and it appeared certain that I would be the next to go. The water was rising in a violent caldron, and I remembered the command that Roland had left with me. *Look to the sky, Alexa Daley! It is there your future lies!* And so I did.

The pillars were set in a wide circle, and I saw the figure of a person diving from the top of the one farthest away. The figure was nothing more than a dot with limbs in the distance, but whoever it was had hold of a rope attached to the closest stone pillar, the one we'd rammed the *Warwick Beacon* into. The very middle was open water — with the pillars all around — and the figure at the end of the rope gained speed and swooped lower toward the water as it came near.

The final mast of the *Warwick Beacon* disappeared and my fingers slipped along the wet rail. Then I felt my legs turning wet, the sea boiling all around me as it took the last of the ship, and I let go, covered by the chill of raging water.

Roland's words rang through my memory: *Come get them! Come and take them now!*

What came next was more a nightmare than reality, and I couldn't tell whether I was awake or dreaming. I only knew that I was rising on the wind with whipping flames grasping at my feet, and looking down I realized the awful truth: The *Warwick Beacon* had vanished, the captain had gone down with the ship, and there was no sign of Yipes.

Tragedy had struck far away from home, and my last thought was the scariest one of all:

I was alone.

CHAPTER 3

THE HIDDEN DOOR

There are very few events that can wake me from sleep experiencing all five senses at once. Having a wet dog lick my face is one of them. There is the smell, sound, and feel of a wide, slobbering tongue licking my face, the sharp smell of a wet coat of fur mingled with warm dog breath, and then the opening of my eyes to find the yellow face of an animal looking back at me, nudging a stick across my chest as if it expects me to play fetch.

"Where did you come from?" I asked. The dog nudged the stick once more and waited. I sat up, took the stick in hand, and waved it back and forth in the air. Nothing about the dog moved except its head as it watched the stick move.

I was in a room that had but one door and one window. The window was high on the wall, too high to see anything but blue sky. The door was only barely open; I could see a shaft of light pouring in, but nothing else of the world outside. The dog, it appeared, had pushed the door open and found me where I lay on the bed. Seeing how wet the dog was made me wonder what sort of place I would find outside. Was I still near the water, or was I atop one of the stone pillars? The only way I was going to find out was by getting up and walking to the door, but I was afraid to go.

As I sat worrying about Roland, Yipes, the sea monster, and the wreckage of the *Warwick Beacon*, the dog barked. He stood up, eyeing the stick, and my heart raced at the thought of who or what else might come through the door.

"Quiet down," I whispered. But even as I said it, I realized that he'd worn me down with those big brown eyes and wagging tail. I stood up and hurled the stick through the high window, watching as the dog darted out the door. Then I heard the dog hit hard and fast into what sounded like deep water.

I crept toward the door and reached my hand out for the polished handle. But the dog was much faster in water than I had supposed, and he bound into the room, dropped the stick at my feet, and shook the water from his body, spraying me from my head to my toes.

"Very nice," I said, picking up the stick. "I wonder if you can find *this* one."

I pretended to throw the stick out the window again and the dog went scampering from the room on wet paws. Then I went back across the room, crouched low, and tossed the stick under the bed. When I stood back up and looked, there was someone standing in the doorway.

"That's not going to work."

It was the voice of a woman. She was silhouetted with light from behind so that I couldn't make out her face, though I could see that she had very long hair. She was tiny, no bigger than me. If not for her voice I might have mistaken her for a child.

"It'll just make him want it more," she told me.

"Where are my friends?" I asked immediately.

The woman stepped to the side of the door and the dog bounded into the room, soaking wet and sniffing. It sniffed the floor, then my leg, then my hand, and finally the bed. A moment later, it had managed to force its sizable head under the frame and emerge with the stick.

"Told you," said the woman. "There's not much you can do now but throw it again. Ranger is what you might call a *focused* animal."

"So I see," I said, and threw the stick out the window. The woman waved me toward the door, but I didn't want to leave the safety of the room.

"Will you tell me where my friends are?"

Ranger returned and this time the woman scolded him gently.

"Leave the poor girl alone."

Ranger sat beside her, dropped the stick, and stared at it sadly. The woman waved me out once more.

"I'm not going to hurt you," she said. "I'm not even sure I *could* hurt you."

It was true that by the looks of her shape in the door I could probably force my way past. I was small but she was smaller.

"Come on," she said, walking away from the door to where I couldn't see her. Ranger picked up the stick and followed enthusiastically. "It's a beautiful day outside. You could use the sun."

"Wait!" I said. I didn't like the idea of being left alone now that I was awake, and I was already growing attached to the dog. There's something comforting about the companionship of animals in a new place.

I walked cautiously to the door and peered out into the light of day, worried by the fact that the woman hadn't answered my question. The house sat unexpectedly on the very edge of a wide body of water. The one-room cottage I'd come out of — if it could be called that — was cobbled together with thin strips of weathered stone and mortar. It had a thatched roof.

"I know it's not much," said the woman. She was standing by the shore with the yellow dog. "But it's home for me and Ranger."

She was about the same age as Yipes, and nearly as little. Her long golden hair ran all the way past her knees. It had a sea-swept way about it, not straight but not curly. Tangled was a better word to describe it, as if it hadn't been combed through in years and years. And she was very soft and pretty to look at. I had the feeling that if I pushed on her nose or her cheeks with my finger, I'd find nothing firm beneath them.

She tossed the stick once more for Ranger and the dog jumped into the water and swam off.

25

"That dog will go all day," she said. "He loves to swim."

A tall, unmanaged hedge thick with green and gold leaves lined the outer edge of the lake where I stood, so that I couldn't see the Lonely Sea below. There were cottages here and there around the lake, poking through the trees in little clusters. Looking up, I saw three stone pillars rising into the air and realized where I was: atop the second pillar, not quite the lowest of the five. I had come into the realm of lost children.

The lake took up a great deal of the space in the middle, and the flat top of the pillar was not as big around as I'd supposed when I'd looked up from below. I moved closer to the woman and saw that she was watching me with bright green eyes like my own.

"I'm Matilda," she said. "I helped save you from the monster that ate your ship."

"But you're so . . ." I'd almost said it. Almost, but not quite.

"What? *Small?*"

"I'm sorry, it's just . . . well it's hard to imagine you could lift me out of the water. How did you do it?"

She didn't answer me as Ranger came back with the stick and dropped it at her feet.

"Where is Yipes?" I asked, "And Roland — the captain of the ship — is he . . . ?"

Matilda pointed toward a weather-beaten rowboat

sitting on the lake. Ranger, taking this as a sign, bound along the water's edge and jumped in.

"The dinner bell will be going off soon," she said. "Can't be late or I'll never hear the end of it from Jonezy."

I looked to my left and my right once more, then out over the lake. I didn't see another person, which surprised me. Did anyone besides Matilda and Ranger even live on the second pillar? Where were all the people who occupied the cottages?

Matilda went to the rowboat and sat waiting. Ranger barked at me, and I knew without the slightest hesitation that if I could understand the dog I would have heard, *What are you waiting for? Get in the boat!*

"There's food on the other side," said Matilda. Seeing I wasn't sure, she added, "And everyone's waiting for you."

It appeared that I wasn't going to get anything more out of Matilda unless I followed her lead, so I gathered my courage and stepped into the bobbing little boat.

Matilda began to row with her rail-thin arms, and I patted Ranger on the head. We were quickly away from the shore, and I gazed into water where only the soft wake of the oars disturbed the surface. Many fish the size of my hand swam under the boat where the water was clear and deep. It reminded me of something else — something giant and scary — that had glided under the *Warwick Beacon* not so long ago.

"You're on the second pillar, Alexa." Matilda could

tell I was surprised to hear she knew my name. "Your friend Yipes told us."

"He's alive — you've talked to him?" I asked, hope rising in my voice.

"I haven't, but I'm told he's doing fine."

I was so happy to hear this news, I wobbled the boat back and forth with excitement.

"Where is he? When can I see him?"

Matilda let go of one of the oars and it dangled lazily on the surface of the water. She pointed into the sky in the direction of two o'clock.

"He's on that pillar, which isn't the easiest one to get to from here. Can you see that long, rising line between this pillar and that one?"

I nodded, seeing what she had described.

"That's a bridge made of ropes and not much else." Matilda wrinkled her nose as if it had tickled inside. "It takes practice to manage a rope bridge like that. And even more practice to swing on a rope from pillar to pillar. We'll work on these things."

"Yipes could do those things!"

If there was one thing Yipes would be very good at, it would be crossing over a rope bridge or swinging on a rope.

"He can climb anything you put in front of him," I said.

"Maybe so," Matilda replied. "But let's talk about that after, all right?"

"After what?"

Matilda wouldn't answer. She wrinkled her nose up and down again. It appeared to be a nervous habit, one that reminded me of Malcolm the rabbit back home.

Why were they keeping Yipes from me? It bothered me, but I was so thrilled to know that he was with me — *somewhere*. It seemed best not to press the point just yet. And besides, there was another, more difficult question I needed to ask again.

"What about Roland, the captain of the ship?" I asked. "Where is he?"

Matilda was quiet. She was rowing again, watching the paddles hit the water so she wouldn't have to look me in the eye.

"He's gone, isn't he?" I asked. "Roland is gone."

Matilda still didn't answer, but she did glance at me then — as if her heart was broken just like mine was. Roland Warvold had indeed gone down with the *Warwick Beacon*. I had counted on him being by my side in this strange new world. Without him, I didn't know who to trust or what I would find on each of the five pillars. It was a scary, lonely feeling.

"It's hard to let things go," said Matilda.

We were very nearly on the other side, and a large group of people had gathered near the shore where we were set to land. I couldn't stop thinking about how they were all lost children from The Land of Elyon. Children no one wanted, children in danger, who had been smuggled to the five pillars by Roland. I had imagined them all at five or six or seven, even if it didn't make sense. I knew many of them had been brought here long before I was born, but until that moment I had always imagined them as children, lost and afraid. It made me want to see Yipes more than ever.

"Matilda?" I said. She looked across at me on the boat. "Why can't I see my friend Yipes?"

Matilda smiled faintly.

"You can see him — I promise." She turned to the water. "Just give it a little more time."

I wanted to object, but we were coming ashore and people had gathered, whispering quietly among themselves. There were three more dogs, happy to see Ranger visiting from the other side of the lake.

I heard a bell ringing from somewhere in a hidden place within the line of trees.

"Just made it!" said Matilda. "Time for something to eat."

As I stepped out of the boat, everyone moved back and parted. They didn't speak to me, but many nodded and smiled weakly. There seemed to be some concern about me. There was an overarching sadness — probably at the loss of Roland. After I'd gone slowly past all the people, a path remained, leading into the trees.

"That way," said Matilda, looking up the path. "You must go to the door."

CHAPTER 4

JONEZY

The door was surrounded entirely by thick bushes so that it appeared to lead not into a house but into an endless wood. I shivered.

"Can I take Ranger with me?" I asked.

Matilda nodded. "I think that's a good idea."

All at once, I had a strange sense that I'd done this before. It reminded me of walking to the glowing pool behind Yipes, of not knowing what I would find there.

Everyone else had moved off, leaving just Matilda, the dog, and me to make our way to the door.

I called Ranger close to my side and felt his fur on my leg.

"Will you go with me, too?" I asked Matilda.

"I think you'd better go without me. But you'll see me again, I promise."

She tucked her long, tangled hair behind her ears and stepped back on the path.

Taking a deep breath, I pulled the wooden latch up and the door creaked open just a little. Ranger nudged his nose against the foot of the door and disappeared inside. It was bright in there — that much I could tell — but a salty wind blew the door shut the moment Ranger slipped through.

"I don't think I want to go through the door," I said, turning back to where Matilda had been. But she was gone. I was alone on the path.

"Ranger?" I whispered, opening the door a crack.

"He's in here."

The voice sounded gravelly and old. It mingled with the sea wind and the sound of Ranger prancing on the floor. I had to push hard on the door in order to get it open against the strong wind, and the moment I stepped out of its way the door slammed shut again. I was standing on a narrow veranda — only a few feet wide — with a rail of stone piled up as high as my waist. Which wasn't high enough, since it was the only thing between where I stood and the open air leading down to the Lonely Sea.

I reached for the door, a strong feeling of danger so very close to the edge, but Ranger was standing at my feet and wouldn't move aside.

"We don't get many visitors here," said the voice.

I turned to my left and my own hair streamed in front of my eyes, the sea wind pushing at the side of my head as if to keep me from the edge. The stone rail ran straight and narrow to a table with two chairs. The veranda was so narrow that nothing else would fit — just the table, the two chairs — and a lone man staring out to sea.

"I saw you coming from a long way out," said the man. "A person can see a lot from up here."

32

He was ancient in the same way that Roland had been ancient. The sun and salty sea air had turned everything about him pleasantly warm. His skin was leathery brown and creased with wrinkles, his hair somewhere between gray and yellow. His nose was straight and thin like an arrow — and, most would conclude, it was a nose of above average length. Like all men who lived on the sea, his eyes were sparkling with life.

"Come sit down. We can eat and enjoy the view. I like company out here when I can get it."

Of all the walks I'd ever taken, this one might have been the scariest. I cannot explain how high up it felt we were, how the pillar seemed to sway in the wind, how low the rail was at my side. A strong gust in the opposite direction would surely knock me off my feet. As if to mock my fear, Ranger put both front paws up on the stone ledge and wagged his tail, barking *Hello!* at the Lonely Sea. I love dogs, but sometimes they do the strangest things.

"Down, Ranger!" I said, a little too forcefully. I was afraid he might push the rail right over. Ranger went back to the door and lay down. This seemed like a good excuse for me to get down on my knees, and so I did, petting Ranger kindly. I was already down there, so I thought it just as well to crawl to the table. This made the man smile, deep crow's feet appearing at the corners of his eyes. When I arrived at the table, I rose carefully to the level of the chair and sat down. The soft swaying of the stone pillar made me feel seasick, and I kept leaning in toward the thick wall of bushes. I realized then that this was no room, but simply a ledge surrounded by trees and brush with a well-placed arch and door.

"Do we have to eat here?" I asked. "It's so close to the edge."

The man stood up and leaned far out over the rail, which scared me half to death.

"A few things I need to ask you first," he said into the rushing wind. "And besides, if you're going to be here a while — which I think is rather certain, given your circumstances — it's best you get used to what it feels like to be near the edge."

He sat back down and looked at the plates before us with his brilliant gray eyes, nodding his chin.

"We have very good fish here. It's even cooked. And the potatoes are not to be missed."

The food did look awfully good, and it made me wonder when I had last eaten anything.

"How long was I at Matilda's house?"

The man thought a moment before answering. It appeared he was having some trouble knowing for sure.

"More than a day but less than two," he finally told me.

"Oh," I responded. I had been hoping for a little more detail.

I decided to try another question. "Who are you?" I asked.

34

He picked some of the fish up off his plate with his hands and began eating it.

"Jonezy. Formerly of Madame Vickers's House on the Hill, presently a leader . . . of a sort," he answered. Then he put another big chunk of white fish into his mouth, chewing it happily. This was *the* Jonezy — the one from Roland's story — the last boy to arrive at Madame Vickers's horrible orphanage before Roland and Thomas escaped. It was odd to have heard of Jonezy as a boy but see him as an old man. Very odd indeed.

"What about Yipes, my friend? Can I see him?"

Jonezy swallowed his fish and cleared his throat harshly, which made his old Adam's apple jiggle up and down. He put his fingers to his mouth and pulled out a long, thin bone. When he was sure there were no more surprises hiding between his cheeks or in his teeth, he observed me carefully.

"You ask a lot of questions."

I felt awkward — like I was in trouble — and I turned toward the door so I could see how far away it was.

"What about if we take turns, you and me?" Jonezy said, seeing that I was feeling uncomfortable. "I'll ask a question, then you ask one. We'll go back and forth. I think we both need some information the other possesses, don't you?"

"Is that your first question?" I asked. Something about that phrase reminded me of Pervis Kotcher, an old friend I hadn't seen in a long while, and I was suddenly sad about so many things. I wanted to cry — probably needed to cry — but Ranger came up next to me and licked my hand. I felt a little better as he looked at me with those comforting eyes.

"He told me you were a smart one," said Jonezy. "I guess I'll have to be more careful."

He nodded toward me, signaling that it had indeed been his first question and that now, by rights, it was my turn. I went easy on him.

"Who told you I was a smart one?"

"Why, Roland, of course. Who else would tell me such a thing?"

He gobbled some more fish, and I did the same. It felt good to have food in my stomach.

"Is that your second question?" I asked through a mouthful of food. Ranger whimpered and I held my fishy hand down so he could lick my fingers.

"This is ridiculous. How am I supposed to get any of *my* questions answered if you keep tricking me that way?"

"That sounded sort of like another question, don't you think?"

Jonezy laughed and nodded in my direction. He was unusual, but I was starting to like him.

"You were one of the first here," I said. "Roland told us your story, about life at the House on the Hill. About how he and Thomas saved you."

"And the giant! Armon the giant. I'd give almost anything to see him again. A remarkable creature."

I didn't have the heart to tell him that Armon had returned to the Tenth City, that he'd never be seen again.

No more soft questions. I wanted real answers.

"Why can't I see my friend Yipes?"

Jonezy ate some potatoes, filling his mouth in order to give himself a moment to think.

"Because we're not sure why you've come here," he finally said. After another pause in which he cleaned the corners of his mouth with his fingers, he added, "Why did you come here, Alexa Daley?"

I did not feel that Jonezy was accusing me, but he was visibly concerned about the answer. What I said would matter a lot. I paused, petting Ranger's windblown fur. My pause lasted too long and Jonezy stood, leaning over the edge of the stone rail once more.

"Roland was my closest friend. We shared many years together and more meals than I can count, at this very table. And I stood here, helpless, watching his beloved ship torn to pieces. There are only two people on the Five Stone Pillars with enough skill to swing that low, and neither are strong enough to carry someone as heavy as Roland."

He turned to me, the sea wind pushing tears along the tracks of his cheeks.

"The Lonely Sea has taken him. And in his place we are left with you and your friend, two people we know little about. And one other."

"What other?" I asked, surprised and heartbroken

37

anew at the certainty of Roland's death. "There were only the three of us — that's all."

Jonezy leaned out over the water again, and this time he pointed.

"That!" he yelled. "The monster that killed the captain and sunk the ship. It remains!"

This was enough to finally get me out of my chair and standing at the rail. As terrifying as it was to lean out and look down, I made myself do it.

"What is it?" asked Jonezy. "What terrible thing did you bring here?"

He was not so much afraid as confused. And I could see why he might be suspicious of me, of Yipes, even against his own better judgment. Roland was dead, the *Warwick Beacon* was sunk, and below us was a monster we'd brought to destroy a place that had always been kept secret and safe.

It was as if Abaddon knew I was looking down at him, knew of my very presence at the edge. There was a great boiling of water at the base of the stone pillar to my left. Then Abaddon's metal arms emerged, snapping with electricity and flames against the base of the narrowest of the stone pillars. Chunks of stone broke free and were hurled into the ocean. The sea monster was ripping the stone pillar apart — and was also climbing! Arms scaled in rusted steel were grabbing hold of the pillar, pulling the full weight of Abaddon's body and head into the air.

This is my home now, Alexa Daley. You and your friends aren't welcome here.

I heard the grave and haunting voice of Abaddon on the wind and covered my ears.

"It does sound awful, doesn't it?" asked Jonezy. "The way it whips those arms into the pillar."

Abaddon drifted back down, laughing in my head, the water frothing angrily until at last the sea monster disappeared. All was quiet again in the Lonely Sea.

I turned to sit back down and found Ranger in my place. He'd eaten all the food off my plate.

"You really have to watch him," said Jonezy. "He's sneaky."

I pushed Ranger gently aside and he stopped licking his paws just long enough to step off the chair.

"Here, take mine." Jonezy slid his plate across the table, but I'd lost my appetite.

"We didn't mean to bring that monster to the Five Stone Pillars," I told him. "You have to believe me."

Jonezy leaned forward on his elbows, taking a wedge of potato from the plate he'd pushed toward me. He popped it in his mouth and spoke as he chewed.

"We're going for a walk, you and me. You must tell me everything," he said, running a sleeveless arm across his mouth. "And quickly."

CHAPTER 5

MY STATION REVEALED

Jonezy stood and pushed his chair to the side of the table. "Follow me," he said. "I don't want to be bothered by anyone until we're at the bridge."

I remembered the looping rope bridge I'd seen leading to the third pillar.

"You're taking me to see Yipes!" I cried.

"Different bridge," he informed me, getting down on his knees and crawling through a hole in the bushes behind the table. He didn't wait or speak any instructions — he simply vanished into darkness. I was again reminded of old feelings — crawling through caves and tunnels, leading to places unknown, following behind those I wasn't sure I could trust. The gust of wind kicked up and pushed against the tall, unkempt hedge. The leaves brushed against one another and made a tangled sound. Ranger barked sharply as if to say, *Let's go, Alexa — standing here isn't getting you any closer to finding Yipes.* And so I dutifully followed, hoping I could build some trust with Jonezy as we made our way. I was surprised to find that Ranger wouldn't follow me after all. He whimpered as I disappeared into the hole, poking his head inside then darting back again into the light of the terrace.

"He won't follow us, and that's probably best," said Jonezy. His voice startled me.

"Why won't he come in here?"

"I'm not sure. Maybe he likes to know where he's going."

"I'd like to know that as well," I said, backing up ever so slowly toward the terrace.

Jonezy laughed and moved on, crawling around a corner where I couldn't see him.

"There's nothing diabolical here, Alexa. It's nothing more than a secret way to avoid being seen. I don't always like having to talk with people. They have a lot of questions."

And so I followed. When I rounded the corner, it wasn't as dark or as small as I'd expected it would be; I was able to stand upright and walk at a slight crouch as thousands of thin shafts of light broke the surface of leaves and branches overhead. Wild tangles of brush grabbed at my arms and legs, but it felt oddly safe and secure. I breathed in deeply the wild smell of trees and flora.

"Roland hasn't been back in almost five years," said Jonezy, slowing down to a leisurely stroll. "I have a feeling much has happened out in the world during his long absence."

Jonezy was keen to know every detail I could give him, interrupting me constantly as I tried to piece together a story of the past he'd had no part in. We stopped many times on the hidden path as we made our way. *Everything* had to be told to quench Jonezy's thirst for information. The whole story of what had taken place beyond the Valley of Thorns in Castalia. All of Victor Grindall's treachery. The loss of Thomas Warvold and Armon the giant. The Bridewell walls torn down. The dark force of Abaddon turned away from The Land of Elyon only to escape into the waters of the Lonely Sea in search of a new home. And, finally, our dreadful mistake: We'd led the monster to the Five Stone Pillars.

After a time of telling, we emerged from the thicket and I found myself standing with Jonezy before a small pond and a set of three windmills surrounded by trees. The windmills were set at different heights and someone was turning a wheel attached to one of them.

"The wind is up today," Jonezy said. The young woman turning the wheel jumped at the sound of Jonezy's voice.

"Why must you use that passage?" she said. "You know how I hate being snuck up on."

She eyed me wearily and nodded in my direction.

"This must be the girl."

Jonezy nodded back but otherwise didn't reply. The young woman returned to her work at the windmill, though she kept glancing back at me as if she were very curious about what I might do. It appeared that she was changing the flow of water, for there was a system in place that took water from the small pond and moved it out toward the edge of the second pillar.

"Tell Miller I'll talk with him about the harvest tonight," said Jonezy, moving off in the direction the water was being drawn. The woman at the windmill nodded once more, and I took it that she and Miller were farmers of a sort, and that Jonezy managed their undertaking.

I followed Jonezy and saw that the water was moved out of the pond and into barrels attached to ropes or vines — I couldn't say which. The thick rope went inside the bottom of the largest of the windmills, where it passed through and circled back. When the barrels went into the windmill, they were empty. But when they came out, they were full of water. The full barrels disappeared through a break in the tree line.

"What a contraption," I said, marveling at the weird system that had been put in place. "Where does the water go?"

Jonezy moved on, through the same opening where the barrels were going, and I followed. We were at the edge of the second pillar, looking across at the lower first pillar in the distance.

"The only water we have is on the second pillar, but we do all our farming over there." Jonezy pointed to the first pillar, which looked very much like a thriving farm of carefully organized fields.

"There's no room to plant crops on this pillar since it's covered mostly with water. But over there, the soil is good when we keep it moist. We use the buckets to send water over and bring crops back. It was made by someone you've never met."

"You mean Sir Alistair Wakefield," I said, sure that this apparatus had been made by the man in the story Roland had told me during our voyage.

"You are such a surprise, Alexa. How could you have known that?"

"I have my ways," I said, feeling mysterious and enjoying it.

"He also helped us devise the ways across, though I don't know if you're ready for that yet."

There were bridges of rope and other contrivances of vines dangling all about through the open air. Some of the ways looked dangerous beyond imagining, and I couldn't see how anyone would use them to cross over.

"I'm the only one left," I said, gazing off at the fields of green and gold below on the first pillar. There was something about the bizarre system of living on these five stone pillars that made me sad for home and the people I'd known. Everything was so alien, so new and different.

"What do you mean?" asked Jonezy.

Somewhere in the telling of the story, I had realized I was the last of the three. No longer was there a great adventurer by land in Thomas Warvold or a marvelous captain of the seas in his brother Roland. Their history had been written and the long-awaited passing of the torch had come. But what was I but a scared child lost in a strange world? How could I replace all that had been lost? Where was *my* place in the world?

I said all these things to Jonezy. When I finally turned away from the first pillar and looked at him, I was taken aback to see a look of astonishment on his face.

"You're Thomas Warvold's *daughter*?" asked Jonezy. "And Roland's niece?"

"I am," I said, surprised by his great interest in this singular point.

"You're sure about this? And there are no others — only you?"

"I'm sure," I said. "I'm Thomas Warvold's only daughter. He has a son, older than me, who lives in The Land of Elyon. But we're the only children he had, and we weren't raised together."

"But why didn't Roland mention you before?" asked Jonezy emphatically. "I know about the son — that he's overseeing kingdoms in Elyon in his father's absence. But you . . . a *daughter* . . ."

"It was a secret kept from all but a very few, to protect me."

"You have no idea," said Jonezy. A grave look clouded his face.

"What are you trying to say?" I asked. "Why does it matter whose child I am? I'm just a girl lost at sea, nothing more."

Jonezy looked positively dumbstruck. He stammered for a moment, trying to find the right words.

"Roland never married," he said. "Or I should say he was married to the sea and no one else. He had many opportunities. A sailor has a certain . . . *appeal*. But no matter how much we hoped he would settle down and start a family, we could never convince him."

I didn't have any idea why any of this was important. I wasn't sure I wanted to know.

"My dear girl, here at the Five Stone Pillars, your uncle Roland was . . ."

"He was what?" I asked.

Jonezy stared at me with those bright gray eyes, the wind whipping hair along his sun-baked forehead.

"We didn't have an official title for him, but Roland made all the decisions. He brought us what we needed and took care of us. He was like a king to us."

I couldn't believe my ears. *King?* How could that be? A king was a great ruler with great power and authority. What did that make me?

"He had no wife, no children," said Jonezy. "I suppose — in a matter of speaking — that makes you a princess, Alexa. What do you think of that?"

My head was spinning. I'm quite sure that if I'd stood up at that moment I would have toppled right over the stone rail and into the sea. Me, a princess? It sounded preposterous!

"But I'm an adventurer, like my father before me."

"Your father before you was also a ruler, was he not?" asked Jonezy.

There was truth in that, truth I'd never thought twice about. My father, my uncle, even my brother — they were all kings of a sort.

"Your uncle Roland brought us everything we ever needed. He cared for us. He had the wisdom of a much older boy from the very start. And when he grew older still, he mellowed into the kindest man I've ever known. He was made to be a king, the very best kind."

"But he was away so much. How could he rule when he wasn't even here half the time?"

Jonezy smiled. "That's the best kind of king, one who's not around all the time."

Even among all the bad news, I couldn't help smiling, if only briefly. Maybe Jonezy was right. In a place like this, it might be best if the king were away a good deal of the time.

"When he was gone — which was often, as you say — we longed for his return. But there was Sir Alistair Wakefield. He was here for a while. And lately I've been watching over things and doing all right."

"So you're the king now?" I said, feeling a little better. "That's wonderful! You're a perfect choice."

"Oh, no, Alexa," he said. "I'm no king. I don't come from that kind of lineage. The Land of Elyon threw me overboard a long time ago. I'm only sitting in, awaiting the arrival of a certain someone."

He couldn't possibly be serious, could he? I breathed deep the ocean air, trying to gather my thoughts.

"Can we keep this a secret," I asked, "between you and me?"

"Why would you want to do that?" said Jonezy. "You're a *princess*, Alexa. *Our* princess. It can't be helped."

I thought a moment, not sure how to respond. Then I remembered why I'd come to the Five Stone Pillars to begin with.

"Roland came back here to bring everyone home, to return you to your rightful place in the world. I believe that's still what he would have wanted."

Jonezy's eyes widened. When he spoke again, it sounded as if he was pleading his case to a higher authority.

"But this is our home, Alexa. It's all some of us have ever known."

"Not everyone," I said. "Some have parents they were taken from. They have brothers and sisters. Remember, not everyone who came here was an orphan like you. A lot were separated from the life they once knew, a life where an evil ruler wanted them dead. That ruler is gone now — all the ogres, they're gone, too. Everyone can go safely back home, Jonezy. I don't know how just yet, but I have to give them that choice if I can. And we have to rid the world of Abaddon, once and for all. Everything will be more complicated if I'm expected to be . . ." I couldn't even say the word *princess* or *queen* or whatever it was I was expected to be.

"I suppose we could keep it secret, if you really want to."

For the first time since arriving at the stone pillars, I felt a twinkle of happiness, if only for a moment. The idea of having free reign of the Five Stone Pillars, of discovering all their secrets with Yipes . . . it was just the kind of news an adventurous girl liked to get. I only wished Roland could be with me to share it.

"You remain as leader for a while longer," I said, then realized I was already sounding as if I'd taken control. "*Please* remain in charge. But give me a guide — Matilda would be perfect — and let me go to my friend. He can help."

Jonezy nodded or bowed, I couldn't tell which. It was awkward.

"Matilda will be thrilled to guide you. It's just the thing for her. Anything you need — anything at all — just ask and it will be granted."

"Some more dinner would be nice, before we go on our way," I said. My appetite had returned. Jonezy nodded and we started back toward the small pond.

"You do realize we have no boat," said Jonezy as we came to the clearing in the trees. "Even if we did, the sea monster would eat it. There's no way off the Five Stone Pillars."

I glanced up into the sky, past the wild line of bushes, to the third pillar rising overhead.

"Let me have a look around," I said. "You never know what I might find."

CHAPTER 6
ACROSS THE BRİDGE
OF ROPES

We returned to the veranda by the hidden path to find Ranger waiting excitedly for us. It was nearing dark by the time he followed me out the door. Either Matilda had returned or she'd been waiting all along, for she stood alone down the path as Ranger bound toward her. I was eager to move quickly — and stop Abaddon as soon as we could.

"You were right about one thing," Jonezy said to Matilda. "This girl is full of surprises."

I glanced at Matilda, wondering why she might think such a thing.

"She has that look about her," said Matilda. "Like she was made for something special."

This made me feel better than I'd felt all day. There's nothing like having someone else think you're special to wipe away all the bad thoughts.

"Take her to your cottage, if you would," said Jonezy. "We'll be taking Alexa wherever she wishes to go in the morning, and I expect that will include places other than the second pillar."

I wasn't sure I'd heard Jonezy right.

"*We?*" I said.

"Well, of course, *we*," said Jonezy. "I want to defeat the sea creature as much as you do."

Jonezy was starting to remind me of Roland and Thomas Warvold, the other old men that had been a part of my life. He was old enough to be my grandfather, and yet he seemed fit and able, ready to take on whatever lay in his path.

"Come on, Alexa," said Matilda. "We better let the old man get some rest. He's going to need it. And so will you."

Jonezy waved us off, went back on the veranda, and closed the door behind him.

"Is that thing still down there?" asked Matilda. Her tender brow furrowed with worry.

"I'm afraid so," I answered.

Matilda took in a big breath and let it out fast, a determined gesture I would come to know well.

"I guess we're just going to have to find a way to get rid of it, aren't we?"

"I guess so," I said, and we began making our way down the path.

There were people waiting at the shore, and there were more dogs, about seven that looked a lot like Ranger and were also grown. Three more were puppies. I picked one of them up, because who doesn't love a puppy?

"Roland brought two of the grown ones here on his last visit," said a man at the shore. He was tall and knelt down beside me. I'd never seen anyone with teeth quite so crooked, but it made him all the more charming with his tuft of black hair and round nose. "He said they came from the City of Dogs. Have you ever been there?"

I looked at Ranger and saw a resemblance to Scroggs, one of the two dogs that had been so helpful in Castalia. How I wished Ranger could speak so that I could understand him!

"I've been there. Have you?"

My comment produced some whispers from those standing nearby, but the man looked at me as if he would give just about anything to get off the stone pillar and go back to The Land of Elyon if he could.

"The last time I saw the City of Dogs I was only six years old," he said, shaking his head and standing up. "I remember there was a broken-down clock tower, but I can't recall anything else about the place."

I put the puppy down and got in the wooden boat with Matilda and Ranger. When we arrived at Matilda's cottage, the sun was just disappearing under the tree line. Soon we were sitting outside under the stars, a toasty fire roasting freshly filleted fish. In the wake of Roland's loss, Matilda and Ranger were an unexpected comfort. Matilda was more like a big sister than a mother, and as we sat by the fire, it was as if she had told Ranger to stay close to me. I sat with the dog's head in my lap, his eyes barely open.

"Are there people on all of the Five Stone Pillars?" I asked.

"Oh, no, only the first, second, and third," she answered, pulling steaming hot pieces of fish from a stick and placing the bits in a wooden bowl. "We took to numbering the pillars long ago. We're on pillar number two. Only pillars number one, two, and three have people on them."

"So the first pillar is for growing things, the second — the one we're on now — is for water and for houses. What about the third — what's it for?"

She passed the steaming bowl to me and I nearly emptied it in three big bites. I was *really* hungry.

"It will be easier to show you than to tell you."

"Is there something wrong with the other two — the ones no one lives on?"

I had the feeling she wanted to say once again that it would be easier to show me than to tell me. I liked that we were reading each other's minds already.

"We can see them all tomorrow if we leave early. How does that sound?"

I nodded, a tingling sense of excitement at the thought of what adventures the morning would bring. I had to believe that the key to defeating Abaddon would lie somewhere on one of the pillars. For now, I had to store my energy and get some rest. We sat quiet for a moment in the night, the warmth of the fire and my full stomach turning me to thoughts of a warm bed. I have a habit of nodding off at times such as these and I don't really remember finding my way to the bed in Matilda's cottage. I only remember waking with a wet dog in my face, the sun rising on a new day, and a feeling of anticipation almost too big for my small frame to hold.

"He loves going across," said Matilda early the next morning. She was kneeling down at the edge of the rope bridge where a basket lay on the ground. Ranger was getting inside.

"No running off," Matilda warned Ranger with a stern look. "You wait for me on the other side like you're supposed to."

Matilda lowered the basket with Ranger in it over the edge of the pillar and it dangled on a long rope — or was it a rope? I'd been trying to figure it out all morning without any luck. When I asked about it, Matilda said, "You'll see — just be patient." All the ropes were softer than any rope I'd touched, and tougher, too, like an ax would bounce right off. And the strangest thing of all was that the ropes didn't have an end — they went right into the ground of the pillar.

"Here he goes — prepare for some barking," said Matilda. She started pulling on a rope at her feet, and Ranger began moving out over the open water. Matilda was right — Ranger barked and barked — but it was a happy bark, like he was looking forward to what was on the other side. It took a few minutes, but the basket Ranger was in finally landed on the other side, where it connected with some sort of pulley and tipped over. Ranger jumped out and barked from the other side.

"Our turn," said Matilda.

Seeing the rope bridge from a distance had been one thing, but standing right next to it was a much scarier feeling. The wind was coming in slight gusts, swinging the long bridge gently back and forth. To be truthful, it wasn't so much a bridge as it was a weird collection of ropes. There was one low along the middle and two higher on each side. Between it all, there wound a web of additional rope holding everything together. It appeared that I'd be walking along a tight rope with extra ropes at each hand to steady my way. It did not look the least bit inviting.

"It's not as bad as it looks," came a voice from behind. Jonezy was walking toward us, meeting us as he'd said he would. "I've done it hundreds of times and only slipped on three occasions."

Seeing that his comment had only made me more afraid, he added, "But, of course, I've never fallen. I'd be dead if that had happened."

"It would be best if you didn't talk anymore," said Matilda. She stood up and went to the bridge, looking out. "All you have to do is never let go with both hands at the same time and always watch your footing. Oh, and don't look down. *Ever*. Follow those simple rules and you'll be fine."

I wasn't so sure.

"Has any part of this bridge ever been broken?" I asked.

"Never," said Jonezy. "It's perfectly safe."

Matilda gestured to Jonezy as if to say, *All right, if you're so sure it's safe, then you can go first.*

"Don't mind if I do," he said, pushing her gently aside and starting out over the water.

Seeing him on the bridge gave me some comfort, because he made it look easy.

"You next, Alexa," Matilda said. "I'll follow close behind."

Jonezy was already well out onto the bridge, his weight bowing the ropes as he swayed gently in the wind. He stopped and looked back when he was thirty steps out.

"What a lovely day!" he shouted. "A little breeze always makes things interesting!"

Matilda rolled her eyes. "Don't mind him. He doesn't get off the second pillar as often as he used to. He makes it sound more exciting than it really is."

She wasn't fooling me, though. I could see that there would be plenty of excitement on the rope bridge as I put my first foot out and held on for dear life. I made the mistake of looking down the moment I had both feet free of the second stone pillar and gasped at the feeling it left in my throat.

"*Uuuuuuuhhh,*" was all I could manage. It felt as if the world had come out from under my feet — which I guess it had. The water was so far below — and, even worse, the sea monster was thrashing in the distance, tearing chunks of stone from the fourth pillar.

"It's okay, Alexa. Just look straight ahead and do what I told you. You're going to be fine."

But I couldn't turn away. My eyes were glued to Abaddon, way down below, and they wouldn't come free.

You'll never make it across. You're going to fall! And guess who's going to catch you?

The terrible voice rang in my ears. How I wished it would go away or that, at least, someone else could hear what I was hearing.

"I'm not going to fall!" I yelled.

"That's the spirit!" shouted Jonezy. It was just what I needed, because I looked up at the sound of his voice. It seemed that as long as I wasn't looking at Abaddon, his voice didn't ring in my ears. It occurred to me that this might be a point worth remembering as I tried to figure out how to overcome him. Would he hear *me* if I spoke? Or was it only the other way around? I made a mental note to test this idea when I wasn't in such a precarious situation.

Matilda came on the rope bridge behind me and Ranger whined loudly from somewhere on the other side.

"Will he be all right?" I asked.

"Don't worry so much about the dog. Just put one foot in front of the other and keep a tight hold. Ranger will be waiting with a stick in his mouth when you get there."

After that, I went along just fine for about fifty steps. The rope bridge kept bending lower and lower, swaying like it would tip right over when a gust of wind chopped through. But I'd gotten the hang of it and felt some confidence as the rope bridge began to turn upward. The third pillar was higher than the one we'd been on by a healthy margin and climbing up the backside of the rope bridge proved harder than I'd expected.

"Hurry up, you two!" cried Jonezy. He'd made it to the third pillar faster than I could believe and was taunting us to join him.

"Don't listen to him," said Matilda. She had stayed right behind me step for step. "Just take it slow and easy."

Something about Jonezy's yelling from above, Matilda's instruction from behind, and the strongest gust of wind yet conspired against my feet. First my back foot slipped, then my front, and then all at once I was hanging by my hands on a swinging bridge a thousand feet in the air.

"Matildaaaaaaa!!" I shouted. My feet were whirling around in little circles trying to find a hold.

"Hang on!" Matilda cried. She reached out and caught one of my feet and pulled it back in, setting it on the thick rope center of the bridge. Then she hopped over my foot and swung out on one hand. She took my other foot and gently placed it back where it belonged. She remained hanging by one arm, and I couldn't believe how strong she was.

Matilda swung around in front of me and settled her feet on the rope.

"Let's finish climbing across before I get us both into more trouble," I said. "I want to see what the world looks like from up there."

The rest of the way was hard going, but Matilda stayed in front of me, climbing backward as she went, watching every step I took to be sure I wouldn't fall. When we finally arrived, Jonezy took my hand and pulled me off the rope bridge. I flopped on the ground, exhausted and out of breath. Ranger dropped a clod of dirt on my stomach and licked my face.

"She'll need some practice on that," said Jonezy. "We might want to send her back the easier way."

"*Easier* way?" I said, sitting up. "You mean there's an easier way of getting over here?"

"Sorry to confuse you, Alexa." Jonezy pulled me up on my feet and Matilda brushed the dirt off my back. "The easier way can't be used to come over, only to go back."

"Oh," I said. My short reply was more of an *ooooooooh* than an *oh*, but it wasn't because of what Jonezy had said. I had gotten my first real look at the place where I'd arrived, staring out over a landscape that was entirely unexpected.

"Welcome to the third pillar," said Jonezy in his very gentlemanly way. I found the scene before me breathtaking, and Jonezy knew it.

"Would you like to take a look around?"

I took a first, timid step forward toward the middle of the third pillar.

"Would I ever."

CHAPTER 7

SKIMMING OVER
THE VILLAGE

There was much about the third pillar that I hadn't expected, but I will begin with the two things that surprised me the most. The first was the shape of its landscape. It was not flat or rolling hills or any of that. Instead it was curved down in the middle — deep and wide — like the inside of an enormous spoon. The whole surface of the third pillar was below the rim, and all of it was alive with a mossy green texture I couldn't help but want to kneel down and touch.

"It's soft," I said, pushing my finger into the bright surface. "Squishy."

"That's because it's full of water," said Matilda. "Pick a spot — any spot — and dig a few inches below the surface. Nothing but water down there."

I had the same boots on that I'd worn throughout the voyage on the *Warwick Beacon*. They were laced up, to keep me warm and dry, but I wished now that I could get them off quickly and sink my toes into the spongy surface of the third pillar. Looking off to my right, I saw that it wasn't all mossy green. There were clumps and shelves of stone scattered everywhere as well.

Before I get carried away with all that I saw of the third pillar on that first day — there is much more to report! — I must first tell the second most surprising thing I saw because I saw it at the rim, before I traveled any farther. The third pillar was almost the very highest of the five, quite a bit higher than the first and second pillars. From here I could see the top of the fourth — the one Abaddon was trying to destroy — and I knew then why no one lived there.

"That looks hard to live on," I said, pointing in the general direction of pillar number four. It was shaped like the opposite side of the spoon, curved at the top, and it was covered in the same bright green moss as the pillar I stood on.

"That it is," said Jonezy. "Its shape makes it dangerous to set foot on, though Sir Alistair Wakefield did it all the time."

Hearing that name sent my imagination reeling. *Somewhere down the path of yesterday, lives the man who never ages, Sir Alistair Wakefield.* I remembered Roland's words as if they were haunted.

"Why did he go there?" I asked. I was also interested in how he'd *gotten* there, since there was no bridge across, but I managed to control my curiosity.

"Who can say?" said Matilda. She was tying her long hair back with a string. "He disappeared onto that pillar for long stretches of time. Sometimes we didn't see him for months on end."

This struck me as odd even for the mysterious Sir Alistair Wakefield. What had he been doing over there?

"That one looks . . ." I didn't know exactly how to say it as I looked up at the fifth pillar, the only one I couldn't see the top of. "A little mean, I guess."

Jonezy and Matilda gazed up at it as well. It was a lot higher than all the rest — shooting straight into the sky — and it was the only pillar with thick black streaks along its sides. What I could see of the top looked like a wall of jagged stone. It had a strange familiarity about it, a little like the walls around Bridewell Common in a day long past.

"*Mean,*" pondered Jonezy. "That's not a bad way of putting it. It's certainly true that no one has ever tried to go there."

"What's its purpose?" I asked.

"Your guess is as good as ours," answered Matilda. "We've simply let it alone all these years. I'll tell you this, though: The walls up there weren't always that high. I remember a time when they weren't even half that tall. It's as if they're alive, growing out of the pillar."

"There's not much more to say about those places," said Jonezy. I could see that he was anxious to get moving. "They're not *for* anything. They just sit there, year after year, with no purpose. Best to turn your gaze in a different direction."

And so I did.

We began our descent into the green spoon of the third pillar, moss squishing gently beneath my boots as we went. This, too, was memorable in a peculiar way. It was like the feeling under my feet on the way to the glowing pool on Mount Norwood with Yipes. Why were there so many things that seemed like copies of places I'd been before? I wondered if it could be that the same hand was at work in both places. The evidence was mounting.

Thinking of all these things made me long to be with Yipes even more. He was my closest friend, my constant companion through so many challenging times. It felt all wrong being away from him in the midst of so much confusion.

There were narrow channels of clear water running everywhere between the mossy green. They reminded me of the veins crisscrossing the backs of my hands. The tracks were so thin that Ranger had no problem putting his left legs on one side and his right on the other, lapping up water as he loped down the hill.

"Where does all the fresh water come from?" I asked, certain that it wasn't saltwater I was seeing.

"Only Sir Alistair would have known," answered Jonezy. "It's a mystery I've tried to figure out for years with no success, and he was maddeningly quiet on the subject."

As we continued down the hill, something else I hadn't been entirely sure about became clearer. There was a village way down below, in the very middle, and it had seemed as if it were shrouded in a covering of earth-toned fog. But the closer we got, the more I realized it wasn't a fog at all, but a weaving of lines running back and forth across the open sky.

"What are all those lines for?" I asked. I could see now that there were ropes like the one's we'd crossed on strung back and forth all through the center of the pillar, like a vast web made by a gargantuan spider. More shocking still, it appeared that here and there people were *riding* beneath the ropes. They were holding on to something between their hands that was looped over the long ropes, their entire bodies hanging down like clumps of fruit, and they were moving unbelievably fast.

"They're skimming," said Matilda. "It's part of our tradition to skim the vines. You'd be surprised how serious people are about it."

"There must be hundreds, maybe *thousands* of vines. It's impossible."

We went farther down and soon we were below the highest of the vines, traveling along a series of stone shelves that wound lower and lower. It was layered for hundreds of feet, this web of ropes or vines that seemed to go on forever. I watched as several more people darted by, flying through the air in the distance.

"But *why* do they do it? It looks dangerous. And it doesn't seem to have any purpose."

"Tonight you'll see it has a very real purpose," said Matilda. She smiled as if she had a secret she was excited to share with me. "The night skim is something that has to be seen to be believed."

The night skim? She had definitely piqued my curiosity.

As we came lower on the hill, I looked more carefully at the scene before me and began to get the idea. The vines ran in every direction above the village. We were coming very near a shelf where someone was about to jump.

"Practicing a little early, aren't you?" asked Jonezy.

The boy on the ledge turned and saw us.

"Jonezy!" he said excitedly. "I haven't seen you for weeks. Where have you been? I hope you'll be flying tonight."

"I wouldn't miss it," said Jonezy.

The boy was clearly in awe of Jonezy for some reason.

"Marco is looking *really* good," Matilda said. "He's been practicing more than ever. Do you think he'll break your record?"

Jonezy sniffed at the air and waved off the idea. I wanted to ask who Marco was, but the boy jumped from the ledge with a howl and zoomed away toward the other side on the rope. He raced over the village, gaining speed until it looked more like he was flying than riding on a rope.

"Very focused, that one," said Jonezy. "He didn't even introduce himself to you. He's something of an admirer. Probably wanted to show me what he could do."

"An admirer?" I asked. But Jonezy was busy watching the boy make for a landing on the other side.

"He's not going very fast," said Jonezy. "And there's no tracer to worry about. We'll see how he does tonight."

It appeared to me as if he was racing over the village faster than I'd ever gone on a horse, which was pretty fast.

"That looks like it might be a good thing to try," I said, mesmerized by the idea of swooshing across open air over the village. In the back of my mind I was constantly trying to devise a plan to defeat Abaddon. Flying over him or down to his level at a great speed might prove useful, and this strange method seemed to hold some promise. Marco had landed way over on the other side and had begun walking across the shelf to another vine. It was the lowest shelf of them all, and this time when he grabbed the rope, I realized it would lead him right down to the ground. He dove into the air, skimming down the vine with alarming speed.

At the very bottom, beneath the random weave of hanging ropes, was a village of houses and paths. There must have been thirty houses or more, all magically clustered around an open field of green at the center. Hundreds of vines disappeared into the ground from every imaginable direction.

"There's no time like the present," said Jonezy as we stood on the slab shelf of stone where the boy had jumped into the air. I'd gotten lost in the view of everything before me and had to shake my head back to reality.

"What?" I asked.

"To give it a try," said Jonezy. "There's no time like the present!"

Matilda called to Ranger. "Go on, boy! Go on! I'll see you at the bottom."

This was clearly a command Ranger had heard many times before, as if it were a race that had just commenced in order to see who could reach the bottom first — Matilda or the dog. Ranger was already gone, racing down the side of the hill toward the village.

"He wins every time," said Matilda. "I think I could beat him to the bottom, but it would crush his spirit."

I had only known her for two days, but I decided then and there that I absolutely loved Matilda. She was everything I'd always hoped for in an older sister I'd never had. Confident, funny, beautiful, small, gentle — she was perfect.

"Will you show me how to do it?" I asked her. Jonezy was a little put off that I hadn't requested his help.

"I feel it's only fair to tell you I was the very first skimming champion on the stone pillars," he told me. He took off his pack and removed a short strand of rope. It had palm-sized knots on either end. "I crushed the competition!" he continued, leaning down and sliding a flat stone near his foot that looked like a dinner plate. Under the stone, there was a shallow hole filled with something yellow and waxy. He held the two big knots — one in each hand — and the length of rope dangled in between until it reached the yellowy wax. Jonezy took great care in rolling the rope with the ball of his foot, covering it with whatever was in the hole.

"What's he doing?" I asked Matilda. We were both eyeing Jonezy as if he were a patient on an examining table. I don't think he liked it very much, but Matilda thought it was hilarious.

"The old champion of the ropes is making his slider extra slick," said Matilda. "I hope he doesn't regret it."

"I'll wait for you on the other side," said Jonezy, putting his pack on with a look of great determination. "In case Alexa comes in too fast and can't slow down."

If I was nervous before, now I was terrified. The idea of losing control and slamming into the other side was starting to set in. It didn't help any when Jonezy tossed his slider over the rope and, with a great howl of excitement, jumped into the air. I watched as he zoomed down the line, faster and faster, his feet held like an arrow in front of him.

It was only me and Matilda now. She could tell how afraid I was.

"Would it help if I told you there was a really good surprise at the bottom?"

"Maybe," I said. "What sort of surprise?"

"Trust me," she said. "This is one surprise you're really going to like."

She had already removed her pack and was holding a slider out to me.

"It's not so different than the bridge of vines," she said. "Actually, there's less to remember. You only have to remember to do one thing."

I took the slider from her, rolling it carefully in the yellow wax.

"What's that?"

"Hold on!"

That seemed easy enough as I held the two knots. They were just the right size, and grooved as if hands had held them a million times over.

"That slider used to be mine when I was your age," said Matilda. "My hands haven't actually grown that much. Not much more than me! But it's a good slider. A *very* good slider."

I heard the barely audible sound of Ranger barking from far below. He was already at the bottom, probably wondering why it was taking us so long. I wrapped the slider over the rope and held on.

"If you want to slow down, just twist it, like this," said Matilda. She took my hands in hers and crossed them, tightening the rope on the vine.

I took one last look at Matilda, gripping the knots in my hands firmly.

"Here goes!" I said, stepping off the edge of the stone platform. And when I did, something very strange happened. I was flying! I mean *really* flying! But there was something important and unexpected about the flying. I wasn't the least bit afraid. In fact, I was laughing out loud as I swooshed over the village. It was a new feeling of freedom I hadn't felt before.

Look to the sky, Alexa Daley! It is there your future lies! Roland's final words rang in my ears and I realized something profound and wonderful: I was *made* for flying! Just as Thomas Warvold was meant to travel by land and Roland by sea, I was meant to fly. I truly wished at that moment that the sky could be my home, that I could always be flying, free like a bird.

All my feelings of purpose and excitement came to a quick end when I stopped laughing and realized I was moving way too fast for a good landing.

"Slow down! Slow down!" cried Jonezy. He braced himself for my arrival, scrunching his eyes and holding out his arms to catch me. I crossed my hands, tightening the slider on the rope, my legs flipping up in front of me and then swinging back. When my legs came forward again, I caught Jonezy in the stomach and he tumbled over backward. I hung from the vine for a moment, suspended in air by the slider. Then I let go and thanked Jonezy for breaking my fall.

"Very good!" he yelled. "Though I think we'll need to work on that landing when time allows."

He got up, brushing himself off. "You must begin the crossover a little sooner next time. Other than that, you were brilliant. Just brilliant!"

Matilda landed behind me, smiling as I was, happy to see that everything had come out all right.

"Alexa Daley," she said. "You're a natural."

"Where's the next one?" I asked, "I want to go again!"

Jonezy led the way down a worn set of cobbled steps where another rope was secured somewhere deep inside the green moss. All of the vines came out of the moss, out of the very pillar itself, as if they were growing.

"How do they stay put without breaking, and how did you make such long vines across?"

"This was all here when we arrived, Alexa," said Matilda. "We asked Sir Alistair over and over, but he would never tell us where any of this came from. It's like a playground, don't you think?"

The vines disappeared into the green moss, to someplace I couldn't see. It was like a perfectly smooth root that belonged in the ground.

"Has one ever broken?" I asked, running my fingers along the slick surface.

"Never," said Jonezy. "If anything, they've all gotten a little thicker and harder over the years. It's like they thrive on being ridden. Some of the best routes — the ones that are traveled dozens of times a day — seem to get stronger and faster every time they're ridden. It's a marvelous thing, knowing these are here for us."

I had a final thought before launching again, and it bothered me a little bit.

"It seems so . . . dangerous. I'm surprised Sir Alistair thought it would be safe enough for children."

Jonezy gazed up through the web of vines. I was coming to see them more that way the longer I looked at them. How else could they keep growing? How else could they be so securely fastened to the otherwise fragile mossy walls? They must run deep *inside* the pillar.

"This was designed by the hand of someone who thought of such things as safety. The higher you go, the thicker the web of vines becomes. I've fallen many times, but there are always many vines to grab hold of as I fall. Every five feet or so, there's a chance to catch another, and they give a little bounce that wonderfully breaks your fall. It's as if whoever made this place expected us to let go, and to let go often. To be honest, sometimes falling is the most fun! Wait until you see a competition — then you'll see some *real* falling."

I was so curious to see a night skim competition I could hardly stand it. But I was also wondering about the surprise Matilda had promised me. I hoped and prayed it was what I thought it would be.

"Let me go first again," said Jonezy. "You have to stop short of the ground or the landing is pretty rough. Watch and learn."

He swung his slider over the rope and remembered something he'd forgotten to say.

"Don't come down until you see a waving hand, all right?"

I heard the sound of Ranger barking from below.

"I'll wait until I see your signal," I said.

74

Jonezy was gone in a flash, standing on the ground below in no time at all. He'd made an expert landing I hoped to replicate when my turn came.

I could hardly wait to get airborne again and I wrapped the slider over the top, waiting impatiently for Jonezy to give the sign. He was waving, but not at me. It was as if he were calling someone from inside one of the houses to come out. And then I saw why he had asked me to wait and what my surprise was. It was the kind of surprise that makes you whoop and holler, and I did just that as I raced down the rope toward the very bottom.

Yipes had come into view, waving both his arms, calling me to come down.

CHAPTER 8

A FEAST AMONG MOSSY HOUSES

In my view, there are many different kinds of hugs. There are the one's you give to huggers, people who hug all the time. These, to me, are by far the least special of all hugs. I see the outstretched arms for the third time in as many days — the expectation of an embrace — and I am drawn in by a feeling of good manners rather than sincere closeness. It's like shaking hands.

There are also those I hug only once in a great while because I hardly ever see them, but who I don't necessarily feel all that close to. Those kinds of hugs are probably the most awkward. I'm expected to hug so I do it, even if I'm not sure I want to. Hugs like these are brief, and I am always left wondering what sort of look the other person had on their face where I couldn't see.

And then there are *hugs*. Like the hugs my parents give me when I'm having a bad day, any sort of hug from Armon the giant, or a hug like the one with Yipes right now.

Yipes and I are not apt to embrace each other unless there's a good reason to do it, but when there is a good reason, it's a hug that feels like it ought to. I know the expression on his face — I can see it behind my own shut eyes. He is beaming from ear to ear, his mouth completely evaporated beneath a bushy mustache that hasn't been trimmed since we left The Land of Elyon. His eyes are closed, too. I've knelt down to hug him and he's trying to pick me up and drag me around. When we let each other go, we both know something special has occurred. The hug has made us truly closer. We both feel better for having done it.

"He's gone," I said, thinking of our lost captain. I had saved my tears over Roland, waiting for someone who could understand the strange emptiness of the world the same way I did.

"I know," said Yipes, pools of water filling his little eyes. We sat down together on the soft green moss and allowed ourselves a good cry. And I knew — just like I knew my own name — that we cried for the same reasons. We did it because we were sad at the loss of our close friend, but we also did it because we were happy. Happy that Roland was in the Tenth City with Thomas, Armon, John Christopher, so many others. And overjoyed that we had each other and a good bit of adventure awaiting us in an unexplored corner of the world. Defeating Abaddon seemed half as hard now that there were two of us.

"You need to trim that thing," I said. Yipes brushed a thumb across his mustache wet with tears.

"Now why would I want to do that?" he said. "This is a mustache made for exploring — nice and thick with the grime of the world. Besides, I've got no one to impress."

"Are you sure?" I said. Matilda had waited at the top for a long pause, but now she was on the rope skimming down toward us. She was small, as I've said. Not as small as Yipes, but close, and so very pretty. The thought had crossed my mind. . . .

"Matilda," I said as she landed and I stood with Yipes. "This is Yipes, my closest friend."

It was the first time since I'd known Yipes that I had ever seen him instantly infatuated. But you don't miss a thing like that.

"A pleasure to meet you," said Yipes, taking off his leathery hat and holding it to his chest. He reached out his hand as if to shake, then pulled it back awkwardly, laughing like an idiot. He ran his fingers through his mustache, wishing it were trimmed and clean.

"How on earth were you able to keep that old hat on in the storm?" asked Matilda. She was trying to downplay her interest, but a girl can tell. Matilda saw someone very interesting before her.

Yipes held the hat out before him, examining it for wear and tear.

"To tell you the truth, I have no idea." There was another bout of silly laughter, and then, thankfully, Jonezy walked up beside us.

"I don't mean to rush you," he said. He was looking directly at me, as if no one else mattered. It made my face feel warm with embarrassment and I worried Jonezy might blurt out something ridiculous like, *Could you come this way, Princess Alexa?*

"You're not rushing us at all." I glanced at my two companions, wiping my eyes with the backs of my hands. Yipes seemed relieved at the distraction. I think he wanted to get me alone and ask me all about Matilda.

"The people in the village have prepared a welcome for you," said Jonezy. "A modest affair, but one I think you'll enjoy. Oh, and we should be getting word any moment now of the enemy's advance. I know you want to be kept aware."

"I'm sure we'd *all* like to know what the enemy is doing," I said. "When will you have word?"

Jonezy began walking toward a cluster of close-by houses and we all fell into step behind him.

"Here comes our scout now," said Jonezy, glancing up into the web of ropes. "Don't mind his manners. He's the best skimmer we've got, and I'm afraid he knows it."

Someone was flying over the village as we walked toward it. Whoever it was appeared to be on a collision course with the thatched roof of the house directly in front of us. And he was going *way* too fast.

"He's going to crash!" I shouted. "What's wrong with him?"

Matilda placed a hand on my shoulder.

"It'll be all right," she said. "Marco can be a little bit of a show-off."

Just when I thought the skimmer on the rope would crash right into the side of the house, he pulled up with his arms, bounced on his slider, and flipped all the way around the vine with a wonderful, spinning motion. His entire body was swinging slow and high over the top side of the rope as he swooshed over the house. By the time he'd cleared the house, he'd swung back down. Then he twisted the slider hard and slowed to a stop, dropping free onto the ground right in front of me with a sly smile on his face.

"Trained him myself," said Jonezy, glowing with pride.

"You'll wear out a slider a week with stops like that," said Matilda. "You should save those moves for competition, not to impress newcomers."

This took the smirk right of Marco's face.

"We'll see whose training pays off tonight," he said, latching his slider onto a belt at his waist as he glared at Matilda.

"Marco," said Jonezy, trying to defuse the rivalry between the two. "This is Alexa Daley."

"Happy to meet you," I said. Marco was young. He couldn't have been more than a year or two older than me. He was wiry and strong, sun-baked from head to toe. His sandy hair looked freshly cut, powdered with blond where the long days of sun and wind had blown the color clean out. He nodded at me without speaking; it was clear he thought an awful lot of himself.

"And this is . . ." started Jonezy, but Yipes jumped in to finish.

"We're already acquainted."

Marco took an immediate interest in Yipes.

"Well, what do we have here?"

Marco acted as if he'd never seen Yipes before, though it was clear the two had already met and developed a dislike for each other. Marco was taller than anyone else in the group — much taller than Yipes — and he acted as if he were measuring my little friend. Yipes only smiled and glanced back and forth between Marco and Matilda.

"Congratulations, Matilda," Marco said. "You're not the smallest one anymore."

Marco thought this was hilarious until Yipes kicked him. Kicking people is something Yipes is very good at, and this was one of his better efforts, in which the toe of his sandal met with the bone of Marco's shin. Marco hopped around on one foot, howling. I think he may have used a curse word, but I couldn't be sure what the word meant because I'd never heard it before. Maybe the Five Stone Pillars had their own curse words. It sure sounded like one.

Ranger came over and stood next to Yipes, licking his hand. It almost looked like Ranger was aware that Marco might try to fight with Yipes and the dog wanted to protect him.

"Let's all calm down," said Jonezy. "The day of a competition is always an emotional time. You can take it out on each other at the night skim."

This seemed to ring true for Marco and he taunted Yipes once more.

"Be careful tonight," he said, shaking his leg in the air to ward off the pain. "It's easy to fall from a slider in the heat of competition. Things have a way of happening."

"I have no doubt," said Yipes.

Could Yipes have already become skilled at skimming? He was a climber — so agile and quick — so skimming would probably come quite naturally to him. I was unexpectedly jealous, wishing they'd taken *me* to the third pillar so that I could have had time to practice.

We had come right alongside the first of many houses. The green moss rose right up off the ground onto the stone blocks, making up the walls of the home, as if it were a home made of nothing *but* moss with rounded corners and arched windows. The roof and door were both of dark wood, made darker still by the blanket of bright color.

"Tell us about the sea monster," Jonezy said to Marco, breaking my train of thought. "What did you see?"

Marco strode over next to us, overemphasizing his limp.

"Whatever that thing is down there, it's angry. But I don't think it's trying to knock down the pillar. I don't see how that's even possible."

"What do you think it's trying to do?" asked Jonezy. It was true that even the narrowest pillar was vast around the bottom. It would take a long time to break it apart, even for Abaddon.

"I didn't get as close as I wanted to. That thing is unpredictable, and I didn't want it snatching me out of the air."

"What does he mean about getting close to the water? Is that even possible?" I asked Matilda.

Marco relished the attention he was getting.

"The same way we rescued you from the *Warwick Beacon*. I swung down."

Marco had been the one to save me! I thought I'd been rescued by one of the adults, but I'd really been rescued by a boy!

For once, Marco did not gloat. Instead, he continued, "It came clean out of the water twice while I watched, pulling itself up, like it was trying to climb the pillar."

All at once, it dawned on me that Abaddon might not be trying to knock down the pillar. Maybe he was smashing holes in it, places where he could hold on with those scaly metal arms and climb.

"How far up did he rise?" I asked.

"Not far. But I got a good look at its head. That thing is gruesome even from a distance!"

"You have no idea," I said, remembering the rusted metal head as it rolled open, the teeth of the monster chomping at the air. *Time to go down with the ship, Alexa. You've served your purpose!*

I shook the words out of my head as Marco went on about what he'd seen.

"It looked like the monster was rising just far enough to punch more holes in the pillar, like it couldn't breathe when it was out of the water and had to go back under."

"Maybe it can't get free!" Yipes exclaimed. "It might want to, but it's a sea creature. This could be good news for us. It may never be able to topple the pillar no matter how hard it tries. And if it can't get out of the water, then we're safe up here. This is good!"

"Don't be so sure," I said. "Abaddon has ways of reaching places he wants to control." He had certainly had no trouble reaching into my own thoughts.

"Abaddon? Who's Abaddon?" asked Marco.

I just shook my head and looked at the house again. I wanted to fill my mind with something beautiful, to get the image of Abaddon out of my head, and the house was so perfect and peaceful.

"Where is everyone?" I asked, aware that this was supposed to be the edge of a village and that there was no one but us. No one was flying overhead. All was quiet.

"They're waiting farther inside, down between the houses," said Jonezy. "We don't see a lot of visitors here, Alexa. They needed a reason to celebrate."

"You didn't tell them, did you?" I asked, sure that Jonezy had let slip that I was Roland's niece.

"Tell them what?" asked Matilda. She was like a

curious sister, afraid I'd kept something from her. I liked the way this felt.

"I'm afraid they do know about the sea monster," said Jonezy, winking at me ever so slightly. "It's not as if we can hide it from them."

Jonezy turned to Marco and told him to go back up to the edge and scout the water once more. The brash young skimmer appeared more than happy to leave as the rest of us made our way into the village.

The houses were set so close to the path that I could reach my arms out and run my hands along moss on both sides as we went. It was a safe, cozy feeling, surrounded by walls of soft color and a blue sky overhead. The path turned sharp, this way and that, and I realized that we were in a labyrinth.

"This way," said Matilda, turning into an opening. A little farther and I couldn't tell if it was houses at my sides or simply stones covered in moss. The walls grew higher and darker of hue, and I was again reminded of a past life surrounded by towering walls I could not escape.

"How much farther?" I asked. We turned another sharp corner and I thought I heard a whisper from somewhere ahead.

No one answered me. They didn't have to, because on turning the corner we came into an open space a hundred feet around. In the middle, there was a long table surrounded by people.

"Welcome to the village at the third pillar," said Jonezy.

Yipes held me by the arm and ushered me all around the table. He had clearly met all of these people before, and being the sociable fellow that he was, he'd already befriended most. There were fish of every kind from the Lonely Sea, apples and pears, and bread!

Here was the greater part of the population of the Five Stone Pillars, and I was somewhat taken aback to realize that there were probably less than two hundred people living here in total. There were children and adults alike, all dressed very much like I was. The same sorts of long shirts of white, brown, and green. I'd changed into sandals for an endless summer that were laced at the ankle. Everything they wore was simple but well made — crafted to last — to get more comfortable with age.

Jonezy must have offered his approval of my arrival, for they never tired of my endless questions, no matter how mundane. In fact, such a clamor broke out every time I asked a new question that Jonezy had to choose who would get to answer me. And so it went something like this. . . .

"How is it that you have bread to eat?"

"Roland brought us wheat a long time ago. We grow it over there." And the woman pointed in a general direction.

"What about the fish? They're so far down, how do you catch them?"

"Roland brought us nets and ropes. We lower them and haul them up."

"And your clothes — they're just like back home. Where did they come from?"

"Roland brought them to us."

It was in this way that I began to realize how important Roland had been to the emerging society on the Five Stone Pillars. No wonder they had treated him as a king — he brought them everything they needed! It made me wonder how the needs of these people would be met in the future. What if all the nets broke or fell into the ocean? What if their clothes all wore out?

It wasn't only me with questions — they, too, wanted to know everything. How did I know Roland? What could I tell them about the sea monster far below? Some, not all, wanted the latest news from The Land of Elyon.

After I'd asked my thousand questions and they theirs (or so it seemed), a group of three girls my own age surrounded me. I was someone new and they all wanted to be my best friend, which I have to admit I very much enjoyed. It was like being a child again at a time in my life when I was sure all the child had drained out of me. There was a moment — like a spark — that felt like I could forget all the trouble in the world and just run free with my friends and be happy.

They took me about halfway up the side of the curved green walls of the third pillar, and we spent the afternoon skimming and laughing endlessly. I could not get enough of this activity and begged to ride again and again until my arms were burning with fatigue. All through the day I flew, looking up and seeing Yipes and Matilda much higher, flying down vines I wished I were skilled enough to ride. This wasn't just fun for me — I was also learning something I knew would soon be very valuable.

Later, when I was so tired and full of food I could hardly imagine doing anything but sleeping, I lay in the open of the green watching skimmers fly over my head through a web of ropes against a blue sky. It was, in a word, magical.

I couldn't have known then that someone was also secretly watching *me*, plotting my demise as I fell fast asleep to the sound of swishing overhead.

PART 2

SIR ALISTAIR WAKEFIELD

He won't be like anyone you've met before.
Best not to keep him waiting too long.
— Armon the giant

CHAPTER 9

THE NIGHT SKIM

"Wake up, Alexa!"

I couldn't say for sure what time it was when I awoke, only that I'd slept clear through the late afternoon and into the early night. Sitting up, I was mesmerized by the world of the third pillar. It had been transformed as I lay sleeping.

"Come on, Alexa!" Crystal, one of the girls my own age, was tugging at my arm, trying to get me up on my feet. "I have exciting news!"

The sky overhead had changed from cobalt to deep blue. At first I thought there were stars hanging close in the sky, brighter than I'd ever seen stars before. But rubbing my eyes and looking again I saw that they were not stars after all, but lamps dangling all through the web of ropes, bouncing as skimmers raced past.

And the skimmers! They, too, were somehow alive with light. They flashed across the sky in every direction like a show of comets and shooting stars.

"What are they doing?" I asked Crystal as she pulled me along the soft floor of the third pillar.

"They're night skimming!" she replied.

"I can see that," I said. "I was hoping for a few more . . . *details*."

Crystal and her friends surrounded me and I was pulled along by the force of the group toward the village.

"We should tell her, don't you think?" asked one of the girls. This was followed by whispering, and Crystal shushing them to be quiet.

"You've been admitted into the competition," she said. She was looking at me.

"What do you mean, admitted?"

"You're going to compete in the night skim. We all begged and begged, and Jonezy said it would be all right. You're in with the beginners, but you're in! It's very exciting."

And I *was* excited! I couldn't wait to get back on the ropes and skim across the sky. And at night! I could imagine nothing better.

"Where are Yipes and Matilda? I want to tell them."

"I'm afraid that will have to wait. They're way up there," said Crystal, pointing into the sky. "The three of them have a duel set to begin any time now."

"The three of them?" I asked.

"Marco," said one of the girls. "He and Matilda have always been fierce competitors, but word in the village is that Marco really wants to humiliate Yipes."

"Where can we go to watch?" I asked, worried about my two friends. "I want to keep an eye on Yipes and Matilda."

We'd reached the center of the village and Crystal glanced into the sky.

"Quickly!" she said. "The sky is clearing of skimmers. The competition is about to start!"

All the girls raced through to the other side of the village until they reached the edge of the hills leading up. I followed close behind as they crisscrossed up a switchback trail toward the top. There were no vines here, as if it were prepared especially as a place to quickly rise along the hill. I passed people going down and saw that others were ahead of us, making their way up.

When I was almost out of breath, we arrived at a long shelf with a twisted rail of wood across the front. Oil-burning lamps dangled here and there around the landing. People were standing all along the rail, talking to one another and yelling out names. I saw Jonezy standing among them and waved.

"So glad to see you awake!" he yelled over the heads of twenty bystanders. "Come closer and bring your friends."

The girls and I scurried across the wide shelf and came alongside Jonezy.

"Look there," he said as I took hold of the rail and gazed out into the open tangle of ropes and lamps. Jonezy was pointing up above us and to the left.

"What are they going to do?" There was a well-lit platform high above us, and three competitors were standing side by side. Even from a great distance, it was easy to see that one was Yipes (the very smallest one),

one was Matilda (almost as small), and one was Marco (about the size of both Yipes and Matilda put together).

"It's a three-part race," said Crystal. "This is the first part."

The sky had cleared of skimmers, and only the gently bouncing lamps remained.

"What about the lamps? Won't they bang into them on their way across?" I asked.

"Let's hope not!" said Jonezy, laughing, but he could see that I was worried for Yipes. "The lamps are not on the same ropes as the competitors are. And Yipes is a fine skimmer. He's a natural."

I was about to ask Jonezy what they were going to do when he stepped away without warning and leaned down, opening the lid to a box I hadn't seen. When his hand emerged, it held a glowing ball the size of his head.

"What is that thing?" I asked. Jonezy handed it to me, and I found that it was heavy like a stone and perfectly round in shape.

"It's a tracer," he said. The palms of his hands were glowing, and as I handed back the tracer I saw that my own hands glowed softly. The stone ball was covered in something powdery and slick that had come off on my palms.

Jonezy held the tracer over his head. Looking up, I could see that the competitors were standing at the ready, arms over their heads, with their sliders held firm over the ropes.

94

Jonezy let out a great cry and dropped the glowing stone over the edge of the rail. All at once, the night became charged with energy from every direction.

I watched the tracer roll along the hill. The hill was uneven where Jonezy dropped the tracer, and the glowing ball curved wildly from side to side as it gained speed. It left a trail of glowing light behind it, and as it went it seemed to grow less and less bright, every side of the stone ball touching moss as it swung back and forth down the hill. The tracer was leaving its glowing, dusty shell behind. We were just to the left edge of the village, and by the time the tracer went past the first of the houses it was impossible to see in the dark. All the glowing powder had been left behind on the way down.

I looked up and saw that Marco, Yipes, and Matilda had jumped free of the platform and were flying down with incredible speed.

"A flag hangs like a tail from each of the lamps," said Jonezy, but I could barely hear him over the shouts and cries from the people standing around me. The shelf we stood on had become a boiling sea of screaming supporters. Some were cheering for Marco, others for Matilda, and a few for Yipes.

"Go, Yipes, go!" I yelled, lending my support as best I could.

As they raced for the bottom, some of the lamps along the way bounced and it appeared that flags had been pulled.

"Pulling flags slows them down," said Crystal. "But they need at least three or they're disqualified."

"What about the tracer?" I asked. The trail of light it had left behind was still there, but it had gotten softer and softer the farther away it was. The tracer itself was nowhere to be seen.

"It's out there somewhere, past the tracer line. Only one of them will find it."

"Go, Yipes! Go, Matilda!" I screamed, my allegiance torn between the two. All the while I kept thinking about how much fun it was going to be when I got my own chance to night skim.

"Marco is going to be first to the bottom," said Crystal. "But he still has to find the tracer."

Crystal was right. Marco was out in front, followed closely by Matilda. I could tell it was her because her long hair was streaked with light as it flew behind her. Yipes wasn't just in third, he was *really* in third, far behind the other two. Marco hit the ground first and began running toward the tracer line in search of the stone ball.

"The ground down below is like a series of soft hills," Jonezy explained. "When the tracer reaches the bottom, it's really moving. The tracer line is long gone and the tracer's not glowing, so it's harder to find than you might expect."

Marco seemed to falter a little, as if he was unsure which way he should turn. I could see his legs as he ran in different directions — Matilda's and Yipes's, too — for they were smeared with the same glowing green dust as the tracer had been.

Matilda was on the ground next, and she took a different route in search of the prize. The two were moving toward the same place from different directions when Yipes appeared overhead. To everyone's surprise, Yipes twisted his slider and slowed down well before the end of the rope. He was hanging overhead, thirty feet off the ground, while Marco and Matilda made a beeline across the moss.

"They've found it!" said Jonezy, and he was right. Both Marco and Matilda sprinted at full speed toward the same spot. "I'm afraid Yipes will have to settle for third in his first night skim."

"Don't be so sure," I said. I knew Yipes well enough to know he wouldn't give up so easily. He was moving very slowly again, skimming right in between and over the top of Marco and Matilda. And then without warning, he was falling through the air.

Everyone leaned out on the rail and gasped. It was at least a twenty-five foot drop. Marco and Matilda dove headfirst onto the moss, arms held out and sliding toward the tracer, but they were too late. Yipes had landed right next to the stone ball and rolled on top of it. He curled around the tracer as Marco tried to pry it away, but there was no use. Yipes wasn't letting go.

The acoustics on the third pillar were very good, like a giant music hall, and we could hear them shouting from below.

"Let him up!" cried Matilda. "He might be hurt!"

Marco stumbled back on his feet and Yipes uncurled. Someone from the village ran out and stood next to them.

"The judge," said Crystal. "He'll sort things out."

A moment later, Yipes was on his wobbly feet.

"Five points to Yipes for retrieving the tracer!" yelled the judge. Yipes held the tracer high over his head and everyone cheered from the rail.

"Five points for Mr. Yipes," the judge continued. "A valiant effort!"

"He cheated!" said Marco. But everyone knew that if you were brave enough to fall twenty-five feet from the air, there was nothing a fellow skimmer could do about it.

"And for flags we have . . ." the judge continued. He counted Matilda's flags, and Jonezy whispered in my ear.

"They're a point apiece and there are ten for each contestant to try for. Yipes could still lose."

"Matilda with eight," said the judge. "A fine effort!"

My heart was pounding as the judge began counting the flags that Yipes had collected.

"And for Mr. Yipes," said the judge, "four flags. That makes nine points with the tracer. Mr. Yipes holds the lead!"

He turned to Marco and began counting flags. The only way Yipes could lose now was if Marco had collected every single one of his ten flags.

"Very rare to collect all the flags," said Crystal. "Very rare indeed."

"And finally for Marco, the reigning champion," said the judge. There was a hush in the crowd. "A perfect score of ten!"

The judge raised Marco's hand high in the air. "Marco is the winner!"

The reaction from the rail was mixed. There were some who couldn't help but admire Marco's skill, but deep down, I think the whole crowd really wanted Yipes to win.

"Your turn!" said Crystal. "Come on!"

Without warning, she took hold of my hand and hauled me along until we reached a ramp up and to the right of the rail. The platform wasn't as high as the one Yipes had jumped off of, but it was plenty high for my first night skim. There were two boys my own age waiting for me, and both appeared more than ready to take on the new girl at the Five Stone Pillars.

I had taken to hanging my slider from a leather belt around my waist as everyone else did. It was a simple matter of taking the center of the slider and pulling it behind the belt until the knots stuck at the top. I reached behind my back and gripped the knots, pulling the slider out of my belt. It was still slick from earlier in the day and I held it over the rope above my head.

Crystal went to the back wall and pulled a small clump of moss from the stones. The underside of the moss glowed with a powdery green and she wiped it along my arms and legs. A chalk dusting of sparkling light ran the length of my limbs.

"Okay," she said, setting the moss aside. "You're all set."

I placed my hands on the rope knots of the slider and held on. I was filled with nervous excitement, my hands sweating and shaky at the thought of diving out onto the vine.

"Off with you then!" Jonezy yelled from below.

I saw the bright glow of the tracer line on the hill to my right and jumped free into the sky, flying down the side of the mountain. Both boys howled with delight, shooting quickly out in front of me. I was so happy to be flying, it didn't cross my mind to reach for a flag until I'd gone past the first two. When I was about to reach for the third, I realized I'd have to hold the slider with one hand, which would tighten the slider on the vine and indeed slow me down. I made the transition, reaching out when I passed the lamp at my side, and *fwump!* I jerked the flag free. I tucked the flag into my belt and went on, sailing for the next flag. Down into the center of the second stone pillar I flew, grabbing flags as I went and wondering where I might find the tracer at the bottom.

100

I was gaining speed, nearly neck and neck with the two boys as we neared the bottom. There was still one more flag for each of us to reach for, but the two boys ignored theirs, more interested in getting free of the vine and finding the tracer. When I reached out and clutched the last flag I felt my slider give way, as if I'd somehow let it slip from my fingers. I was still fifty feet from the ground and felt a chill of fear at the thought of falling so far. There were vines zigzagging like a web beneath me, and I would have to reach out and catch one with an arm or a leg in the dark. It wouldn't be easy.

I still had a hold of the flag and when it popped free from the lamp I careened through the open air. I missed the first safety vine, but I caught my legs from the back on the second rope. I found that it rather gently broke my fall and bounced me up and down until I was hanging upside down in the air like a sleeping bat in the night. The judge came running up beneath me, and glancing over his shoulder I saw that Ranger was in hot pursuit. The dog had run down the hill and was nearing the field.

"Catch!" cried the judge, throwing me a new slider. It flew toward me in the night air, flipping and spinning as it came. When it was within an arm's length, I lashed out and caught it.

"The competition continues! You're docked one flag for falling, but you may yet find the tracer!" cried the judge. He ran off toward the edge of the field as if this were a more common occurrence than I'd imagined. I flipped up on the vine and attached the new slider, but I'd lost all my momentum. I drifted down the rope slowly, taking in the view of everything below.

Ranger had made it down the hill and was racing toward me. The two boys weren't much more experienced at finding the tracer in the dark than I was, and they ran around in circles trying to find it. People were yelling down and pointing, but this was of little help. Finally, one of the boys shouted that he'd found the tracer and the judge ran out onto the field again.

By the time I touched bottom, Yipes, Matilda, and Jonezy had caught up. Ranger had fallen behind, searching the field for something in the dark. A group of girls led by Crystal were making their way down the hill, still well off from the field.

"What happened up there?" asked Jonezy, gasping for air. He was the oldest by far, and it had been a long run. "You were skimming so beautifully and then . . ."

"I guess my hands must have slipped," I said. "I don't remember exactly. It happened so fast."

"It looks as if you got five flags," said Yipes, counting them where they hung from my belt. He knew how to make me feel better at a moment like this. "That's one more than I got!"

"I'm just glad you're all right," said Jonezy. He looked at Matilda. "Maybe a bit more practice on holding the slider would be worthwhile before she competes again."

Ranger came bounding up beside us as we spoke. He had something between his teeth, which he dropped at my feet, barking for me to throw it for him.

"What have you got there?" I asked the dog, picking it up. To my surprise, it was exactly half of my slider. It had been torn at the middle, and I held it by the one knot that remained.

"That's odd," I said.

"Let me see that," said Matilda. She took the broken slider in her hand and examined it carefully as Jonezy looked on. The two glanced at each other with some concern.

"What is it?" I asked. "What's wrong?"

Matilda hesitated, but Jonezy nodded as if to say it was all right.

"Someone wanted you to fall."

"What do you mean, *wanted* me to fall?" I asked.

Jonezy looked back and saw that Crystal and the other girls were about to arrive and make a fuss over me.

"I think it was a warning of some kind," Jonezy said quickly. "No one dies falling on a night skim. There are too many vines to take hold of on the way down. But you might have been hurt, or scared off."

Yipes was the first to react, and it was clear to everyone that he thought Marco was responsible.

"Where is he?"

Matilda couldn't help a smile at the scowl on Yipes's face and his tiny raised fists. He was fighting mad, and there was something about a very angry Yipes that was hard to take seriously.

The girls arrived and a clamor ensued, but even through all the noise they were making I was aware of only one voice. It was the sinister voice of Abaddon in my mind, a voice only I could hear. It was calling from somewhere far below.

How I love to toy with you, my little princess. It warms my cold heart at the bottom of the Lonely Sea! You should pay more attention to me. Soon I'll rule this place, and you'll be the same as Roland — a distant memory.

CHAPTER 10

RETURN TO THE HOUSE ON THE HILL

Jonezy could see that the fall had rattled me, and after a few minutes he shooed Crystal and the other girls away. They ran off, disappointed that I would not be joining them, but equally excited about all the races yet to be run in the night skim.

We moved off on the opposite side of the hill and soon we were in a private place that looked out over the competition. We sat together — Yipes, Jonezy, Ranger, Matilda, and myself — on a soft patch of level moss high on the hill. That is, everyone but Yipes sat. He paced, mumbled, and once in a while raised his fist in the air and yelled into the night where no one but us could hear him shouting.

"Coward!"

"Lunatic!"

"Brute!"

Matilda and I looked at each other just exactly like I thought two sisters should. There were unspoken words between us, but we each knew what the other was thinking.

You like him, don't you? These were my unspoken words.

I do. He makes me laugh. These were hers.

We need to calm him down. These unsaid words belonged to us both.

"I'm fine," I said. "There was never any real danger. Like Jonezy said, he was only trying to scare me. And honestly, we have more important things to talk about."

Yipes begrudgingly sat down with the rest of us and Jonezy breathed deep the night air.

"This is my favorite place to watch a night skim," he said. Lamps sparkled and bounced above and below as competitors zoomed down vine courses. "The lights and the sounds are marvelous from here, but it's private and peaceful, too, away from the crowd."

There had been something on my mind off and on all day, and hearing Abaddon's voice at the bottom of my skim had spurred me to ask about it.

"Don't you think we should be doing something more about the sea monster?" I asked. "It's still down there, trying to climb up one of the pillars."

Jonezy rubbed his temple and the ends of his fingers disappeared into wisps of hair.

"Let's enjoy this one night, shall we?" he said at length. "Tomorrow will come soon enough with its sea monster and its many worries."

I felt he was trying to escape the unavoidable.

"But we're wasting valuable time. We should be *doing* something."

"What would you like us to do?" asked Jonezy. He

was staring at me as if this were a challenge, like he wanted to see how I would handle a sea monster if I were in charge.

I hesitated, both unsure of how we should proceed and unwilling to hint to Yipes and Matilda that I actually *was* in charge.

"You're full of energy, Alexa Daley," said Jonezy. I felt a Thomas or Roland Warvold speech coming and wanted to plug my ears. "But sometimes you have to wait for an answer to come to you. Especially when the questions are difficult ones."

"What's that supposed to mean?" I asked.

"The truth is we're not equipped to fight off an average-sized lobster, let alone a sea monster bigger than the *Warwick Beacon*. No one here is trained to fight. There are no weapons, unless you count fishing nets and wooden harpoons. There's never been any reason to protect ourselves. We must come up with a plan, and I know you will be a major part of it."

He gazed out into the night skim with some nostalgia.

"It would be a shame to lose all this. It's a beautiful place."

He glanced back and forth between Yipes and me.

"Do either of you have any experience with this sort of thing?"

It occurred to me then that maybe Roland had planned our coming here all along. I certainly wouldn't have put it past him. Maybe he knew Abaddon would follow him to the Five Stone Pillars no matter when he chose to go, and that was why he'd waited as long as he did. But he couldn't wait forever. He had to return at some point, and who better to bring along than two people who had already been caught up in a great fight against an evil force?

Yipes took this moment as an opportunity to impress Matilda.

"Now that you mention it, I have been in a skirmish or two."

"Have you now?" said Jonezy, looking at Yipes as if he was hard-pressed to believe someone of Yipes's stature could carry a sword, let alone carry the day on a distant battlefield.

"It's such a perfect night," said Matilda. "What about a walk before talking about weapons and fighting off monsters."

She was looking directly at Yipes with an expression that asked, *Will you walk with me?* But for all his adventurous experience, Yipes seemed not to understand. So I kicked him and nodded in Matilda's direction.

Yipes looked at me, then at Matilda. He took off his hat and said, "I'd be delighted to take a walk."

Matilda jumped to her feet and moved off without him; Ranger pranced alongside.

"Yes, that's just the thing," he said, getting up himself. "A walk will do us good."

I shooed him with my hand, and a moment later Jonezy and I sat alone watching the skimmers zoom across the open expanse of the third pillar. After a long silence, he spoke.

"I remember Thomas and Roland when they were your age," he said. "They looked a lot like you then. Bright eyes full of longing — eyes that wouldn't rest until they had lit on some means of escape. I was a shy boy when I met them, and small besides. I was frightened half out of my mind when I arrived at the House on the Hill, but I knew right away when I met the Warvolds that Madame Vickers and that terrible boy of hers — Finch was his name — could never hold them. I felt sure that my knowing them would be brief, that they would soon be gone. And so it came to pass."

The story of Thomas and Roland leaving the House on the Hill weaved its way across my memory.

"What else do you remember about that time?" I asked, curious about a past I knew so little about. "What else do you remember about *them*?"

"They didn't smell very good," said Jonezy, smiling weakly in the dim light of the third pillar. After a moment, he turned more solemn. "I remember a certain feeling that has never gone away. Back then, everything before me was misery and fear, but when I looked at Thomas and Roland, I knew everything would be all right. They had that effect on everyone around them.

After they left, a lot of the children lost hope, but I didn't. I knew someday Thomas and Roland would return to rescue us."

Jonezy had been looking down at the racing skimmers, but he turned to me now.

"And, of course, they did. They returned with Armon, and then Roland and Sir Alistair took us far away across the Lonely Sea. Now all of them are gone — Roland, Thomas, Sir Alistair Wakefield. All gone, as you so rightly put it, into the secret realm of the Tenth City.

"There is a new evil that threatens to overtake me — to overtake everyone. The problem with those of us who came here from The Land of Elyon so long ago is that we weren't meant to lead but to follow. It takes both kinds. And so this is a time that feels familiar to some of us — as if the world is about to turn dark and dangerous."

"I wish I could go back and change everything," I said.

"No need to do that," said Jonezy, standing and taking his skimmer out of his belt. "Seeing you here now, I have that same feeling I once did — that everything will be all right."

"You shouldn't count on me for anything," I blurted out. "I'm not like them."

No matter how many times the world had attempted to show me how special I was, I had always remained sure that it was all a hoax, that I really wasn't special after all. That I had nothing to offer.

"Well, you certainly do have that look in your eyes," Jonezy observed.

"What look do you mean?"

He watched me intently, holding the knots of his skimmer in his hands.

"The same as them, as if you'll find a way off the stone pillars no matter who tries to keep you here. And you smell a lot better than they did way back when, which is a nice change for the better."

This made me smile as I watched Jonezy walk a few steps to the nearest vine and toss his skimmer over, looking for all the world like a young champion about to fly for the bottom.

"You know, Alexa," he said, "there are a lot of people who don't want to leave this place. Take Marco, for instance. He was born here. He's never seen the land of his ancestors. This place is his home. Seeing you makes him nervous about the future."

"But why? I can't imagine how I'm ever going to leave this place, let alone take anyone with me against their will."

But Jonezy was already gone, racing for the bottom with a howl of laughter. I was left alone with my thoughts, which quickly went from all the big things we'd talked about to the simple pleasure of skimming. I was fantasizing all about how I'd taken every one of my ten flags and the tracer ball, too, when Matilda and Yipes appeared out of the darkness. I jumped to my feet.

"Jonezy's gone thataway," I said, pointing down to the village. Ranger tossed half of my old skimmer at my feet and barked. I picked it up, tossed it, and watched Ranger chase after.

"Where did you walk to?" I asked.

Yipes and Matilda kept glancing back and forth at one another in a way that told me there was something else on their minds. Yipes finally broke the silence.

"Matilda and I have been talking."

Matilda put a hand on my arm.

"You can't tell anyone."

"Tell anyone what?" I asked.

Matilda looked down the hill in the direction Jonezy had gone to make sure we were alone.

"Come on," she said. "There's something I need to show you."

She walked up and out of the third stone pillar, all the way to the very edge.

"Is this where you walked before?" I asked Yipes.

"It is," he answered. "Only a little farther."

I tossed the broken skimmer down the side of the mossy hill and Ranger darted off once more. It was growing darker the farther we moved away from the night skim, and Matilda bent over, tearing a chunk of moss from the ground. The underside glowed a whitish green and gently illuminated our way. We were closer to the edge than I'd thought.

"Is it safe to be so close?" I asked. "What if a gust of wind comes up and blows us off?"

Winds on the Lonely Sea could be unpredictable. I could easily imagine being picked up off my feet and carried out over the water.

"This is far enough," said Matilda. "We can see it from here."

"See what?" I asked. Ranger was back, nudging the skimmer closer and closer to my foot to get my attention.

"There," said Yipes, pointing out where the light shone.

Sitting on the border of the third stone pillar was a great pile of rope that looked as if it hadn't been touched for a long time.

"What is it?" I asked.

There was a pause in which Ranger barked for attention, but I didn't take my eyes off Matilda.

"It's a way across, to the fourth pillar," said Matilda. "A way to some answers."

I picked up the skimmer once more and threw it back into the darkness as hard as I could.

"That's where Sir Alistair Wakefield disappeared to for long stretches of time?" I asked.

"The very place," said Yipes.

"There was once a rickety rope bridge that ran across,

hardly ever used," Matilda explained. "Roland he rope a long time ago, because there were no ading across. Sir Alistair Wakefield didn't want an e to know what he was doing. And then, after he was gone, the children used to dare one another to go across. It was too dangerous, so the bridge was cut."

"Have you been there, to the fourth pillar?"

"Only once, a long time ago. I didn't find anything but dirt and rocks, and it's not an easy place to explore because of its shape. It would be easy to roll down the hill and fall off."

"But maybe if the three of us were to go together, it would be okay," said Yipes. "He had to have a secret place where he spent all that time, someplace we can't see. Maybe there's something hidden on the fourth pillar that will help us."

"We'll have to wait until morning, when there's light," said Matilda. "It won't be easy, but I think we can get across."

I looked again at the coil of rope and couldn't envision how we'd ever get across. Ranger appeared with the skimmer and we started back in the direction of the night skim. We watched a while longer, then Yipes left me and returned to the village beneath the web of ropes in the sky. He had settled into a small cottage there that reminded him of home. Jonezy, Matilda, and Ranger accompanied me back to the second pillar. And it was easier getting back — *a lot* easier, as they'd said it would be. There was a nice and thick vine running down to the second pillar. Because it was lower than the third pillar, we were able to skim over the water after Ranger went across in the basket.

"There's something different about you," Jonezy said as I touched ground behind him on the second pillar. "What are you up to?"

"I can't imagine what you're talking about," I said. Matilda and I had agreed not to tell Jonezy about our plan just yet. If there was nothing to be found on the fourth pillar, there was no reason to worry him, and Matilda didn't think he would let us go if we said anything about our plans.

But Jonezy had been right to spot the familiar Warvold sparkle in my eye. The rope was a beginning, but how was it used? And if we could get there, what secrets would we find on the fourth pillar?

CHAPTER 11
FLIGHT TO THE
FOURTH PILLAR

The next morning, Ranger woke me at the crack of dawn. He was wet as usual, but it wasn't the smell of a wet dog that woke me up this time. Ranger had slept in front of the door, wrapped snuggly around the broken skimmer from the night before. He had set the skimmer quietly and carefully in front of my face, nudging it forward until it touched my nose.

"What are we going to do about this dog?" I said, wiping the smell of slobber off my face. Matilda was sleeping next to me — it was her bed, after all — and I heard her stir and sit up.

"I wish I knew," she said. Then I looked at her and laughed out loud.

"That's quite a head of hair you've got," I said.

I could only see her nose. Everything else was covered in a tangled cloud of curls. She parted the spirals of hair that ran like a mop over her face and peered out.

"It's cozy in here," she said. Then she rolled off the bed, walked out the door, and jumped in the lake.

When I heard the splash, I sat up and felt just how sore I was. My shoulders and arms were tender and aching. I hadn't realized how much strain skimming had put on my body.

Matilda came back, dripping wet in her shorts and shirt.

"Don't do it," I said. But it was too late. She had hold of her long hair and was ringing it out over my head.

"Feeling a little sore, are you?" she asked, taking notice of the way I was rubbing my own shoulders.

"Very sore, actually."

"Well, there's nothing like an exploration to cure a little pain. Let's go find Yipes."

We ate smoked fish and also grapefruits, though we didn't really eat the grapefruits so much as drink them. Matilda showed me how to cut a small hole through the peel, then squish the grapefruit in my hand as I turned it in a circle. When I put my mouth over the hole in the peel and tipped the grapefruit up in the air, I enjoyed the sweet and sour taste of cool juice.

We expected to return by nightfall, so we brought only what we absolutely felt we would need — two grapefruits, water in a familiar-looking jug, some dried fish, a small knife, and a length of rope.

"Don't spend the whole day howling your head off," said Matilda. She was down on her knees with her arms around Ranger. "Go visit Jonezy. He'd love to see you."

Ranger barked as if he was about to go on a big

adventure, but we couldn't take him with us. He'd have to stay behind whether he liked it or not.

I felt a new sense of confidence as we set off. I had my bearings and knew where things were. I knew the way to the first pillar with its groves of trees and fields of crops. I could see the third, fourth, and fifth pillars standing in a row before me. The thoughts of seeing Yipes in the village and sneaking in a run or two of skimming made me happy. I was starting to get used to this place, and I was desperate to find a way to save it from Abaddon.

Soon we were crossing the vine bridge, listening as Ranger whimpered to be included. He was still barking loudly when we reached the other side and dipped down into the skimming pillar. I had the great thrill of skimming down to the village, the wind bringing little tears to the corners of my eyes.

"I wonder if Yipes is up yet," I said when we came to the village of cottages at the bottom and worked our way through the winding paths. It was very early, only an hour past sunrise. "It can be challenging to wake him."

A familiar but unwelcome voice came from the windowsill of a house we passed by.

"You're wandering around early this morning."

It was Marco, sounding as bothersome as ever.

"Looking to get in some practice before the next night skim?" he asked in a most unfriendly tone.

"I know what you did," I said, glaring in his direction.

"You mean the little mishap with your slider last night? I can't say that it surprises me. After all, you did bring that monster to our doorstep. What sort of welcome did you expect?"

"You're terrible!" said Matilda. "And you should be ashamed of yourself for putting any skimmer in danger."

"So long as we're accusing each other, maybe we should ask Alexa what happened to Roland Warvold. What do you say, Alexa? What happened out there on the Lonely Sea?"

I kept walking, angry enough to punch him and knowing I'd better keep moving.

"And by the way," cried Marco, leaning out the window, "say what you want, but I didn't cut your slider."

"You expect us to believe you?" I yelled back. "Everyone knows you hate Yipes and me. Just leave us alone!"

Marco was about to say something else, but other heads were popping out of windowsills and looking on, wondering what all the fuss was about. I felt badly that we'd made so much noise so early, especially after the night skim, which had gone very late the evening before.

"This way," said Matilda, taking me by the arm and leading me down a path that led to a cluster of small cottages. "He's just afraid of what changes are coming. Give him some time."

"Time for what? To devise another way to get rid of me?"

We came to the windowsill of the smallest cottage of them all, and Matilda leaned her head inside.

"He's snoring," she said.

I was still upset and didn't answer.

"Wake up, Yipes," Matilda said in a soft voice.

"That won't work. You'll need to hit him over the head with something heavy."

Matilda looked at me like I was really overdoing it, and I realized how childish I was acting.

"Don't let Marco get to you so much," she said. "He would never do anything to *really* hurt you. He's not that bad."

I walked to the door that led into Yipes's cottage and pushed it open on squeaky hinges.

"Doesn't anyone live here?" I asked, curious why it had been empty before Yipes arrived.

Matilda looked awkwardly at me for a moment before answering.

"This is where Roland Warvold used to stay when he came to the third pillar. There's another place on the first pillar where he also lived, but sometimes he liked to come here and watch the skimmers. He liked that he couldn't see the Lonely Sea from down here. It seemed to take his mind off things after a long journey."

The cottage took on a new meaning for me then, and looking inside I had a deep sense of longing for Roland to return. It was so simple inside — hardly anything at all. I walked in and saw that there was a chair and a table set neatly with things to write letters. And there was a drawing pinned up above the desk. It was of two small figures standing before the towering Wakefield House.

"I know that place," I whispered. Matilda peered in through the windowsill from where she stood outside.

"Have you been there?"

"Only in my dreams, but Roland told me all about it. Those two figures, those are Roland and his brother Thomas when they were boys. I think Thomas must have drawn it a long time ago."

I stood looking at the drawing and the desk, feeling the sadness Roland must have felt. His long separation from his only brother and the long days passed on the stone pillars or out at sea. Adventure, I knew, could be lonely sometimes.

I took a pen from the writing table. It was the kind that needed to be dipped in ink in order to work, but it had long since dried up. It was sharp as I touched it to my finger.

"You wouldn't dare," said Matilda.

"Oh, but I would! He should have been up an hour ago, and instead he's making us wait. I think he deserves a little prod to get him up and moving."

I crossed the room and looked at Yipes. He was really snoring up a storm, and his shoeless toes were sticking straight up in the air. I poked his big toe with the pen, probably a little harder than I intended to.

"Back, you beast! Back!" he cried, sitting up in bed. Then he flopped back down and began snoring again.

"Unbelievable," said Matilda.

I poked the pen into Yipes's big toe once more, and this time he rolled over and fell out of bed. Hitting the floor seemed to do the trick. He wobbled back and forth, yawned, and rubbed the sleep out of his eyes. When he saw it was me, he smiled.

"Good morning, Alexa!" he said, standing and rubbing his shoulders, which must have ached as much as mine did. He took an old hanky from his pocket — one he'd carried all the way across the Lonely Sea — and he blew his nose with great enthusiasm.

"Where's Matilda?" he asked.

"She's watching you from the windowsill."

Yipes turned and saw Matilda, who smiled and waved good morning.

"Oh!" said Yipes, hastily wadding up the hanky and stuffing it into his pocket. "Good morning, Matilda. I didn't see you there."

There was more chatting as Yipes gathered his things and we began our journey to the outer edge of the third pillar. It wasn't so very far, but it was an uphill climb all the way, and we stopped at three or four stone shelves as we went. Each time I wanted to turn around, take my skimmer in my hands, and fly down the vines that hung ready to be ridden. And each time, Matilda reminded me that we had to keep moving, that there was an even more thrilling flight awaiting us at the edge of the third pillar.

When we were near the top, I looked back and saw

that someone was following us from a distance. The figure was yelling something, but I couldn't hear what it was. It might have been Jonezy or Marco, but either way, they were at least twenty minutes behind us.

"Hurry now," said Matilda. "We don't want to have anyone trying to stop us."

"Are you sure we shouldn't wait?" I asked. "I think it might be Jonezy trying to tell us something."

"If it is Jonezy, he'll only try to stop us from going," said Matilda. "He'll think it's too dangerous."

Yipes looked at me and gulped nervously.

"*Is* it too dangerous?" I asked. We had arrived at the coiled rope, and Matilda was examining it.

"It's different than skimming," she said. "And, yes, it is dangerous. Especially given our new guest at the bottom."

I wasn't close enough to the edge to peer down and see if Abaddon was still there, but it seemed very quiet and still on the Lonely Sea, so I got the feeling the monster was not in sight.

"This rope is what remains of the bridge that once spanned the distance between here and there," said Matilda, pointing across to the fourth pillar. We weren't standing directly across from it. Instead, we were back a few hundred feet along the rim of our own pillar.

"The rope is attached way back there," said Matilda, pointing this time down the long line that ran off into the distance along the edge. "If my calculations are right, we should be able to jump here and the rope will carry us on an arc to the bottom, then lift us high enough to grab hold."

"Grab hold of what?" I asked. Yipes was being awfully quiet while I questioned Matilda, which made me think he'd already been through all this with her the night before. My suspicions were confirmed when Yipes spoke up next.

"On the other side, part of the old rope bridge remains."

Hanging down like the long tail of a giant dog were the frayed remains of rope and wood planks on the fourth pillar.

"I'm going to swing across and attach this rope to the other side," said Matilda. "I'll climb partway up and then the two of you can skim across the open sea."

I started to protest — it sounded extraordinarily risky — but Matilda seemed sure she could do it.

"Do you remember when the *Warwick Beacon* came under attack?" she asked.

I nodded, knowing what she would say next.

"I was able to swing down and get hold of Yipes, and this will be easy compared to holding on to him while I was hauled back up to the second pillar."

I wished Matilda had been the one to save me, not Marco. I had to imagine that he regretted his decision now.

Yipes had been very quiet while Matilda and I had

talked. Turning to the edge, we both saw at once what he was up to.

"I'll see you on the other side!" he cried. "Wish me luck!"

And then he ran along the rim of the third pillar and jumped into the air, the rope held firmly in his hands.

"Yipes!" Matilda and I screamed at once. We both got down on our hands and knees and crawled to the very edge of the pillar, terrified at what would become of Yipes as he sailed down toward the Lonely Sea. We saw that he was free-falling, gaining speed as he descended along the rock wall of the pillar. If not for the fact that all the pillars curved in at the middle in varying degrees, he would have almost certainly been dashed against the cliffs leading up as he sailed past.

"Why would he do that?" said Matilda.

"Because he likes you. He doesn't want to see you get hurt."

"But . . ." said Matilda, unable to think of anything else as she watched the rope unwind from its coil with a loud whishing noise.

"I think he'll be all right," I added. "He's good at things like this. You should see him climb a tree."

The coiled pile of rope came to an end and the long line that ran across the third pillar began to disappear over the edge, pulled down by the falling body at the other end. The remains of the rope bridge on the other side ended lower than the top of the third pillar where we waited. It had been cut free from the third pillar, and the whole of the bridge hung lifeless on the other side. If only Yipes could attach the rope he sailed on to the bottom of the bridge, Matilda and I could skim to the other side. After that it would only be a matter of climbing what amounted to a long ladder up the side of the fourth pillar and taking the rope with us. Once we reached the top, we'd be above the third pillar again and we could skim back across. As long as one of us remained on the fourth pillar, we could get back and forth in this way. But the most dangerous part was under way — getting the rope across for the first time — and Yipes had taken it upon himself to accomplish this perilous task.

"This is the really important part," said Matilda, watching Yipes intently. "There's going to be a lot more force on the rope than he realizes when it catches and he swings up. He may not be able to hold on."

And just then, as I should have expected, the voice of Abaddon was ringing in my ears.

Wait until you see how far out of this water I can come. Say good-bye!

"NO!" I cried, inching forward.

"He's doing fine, Alexa. He's going to make it!"

"You don't understand!" I screamed.

As Yipes reached the very bottom of the length of rope, he was nearly halfway down the side of the third pillar. The fourth pillar was taller than the third, but even with the extra length, he seemed shockingly close to the Lonely Sea as he started swinging back up on the other side.

Abaddon was watching, for he burst violently from the water, timing his ascent to match the lowest point of Yipes's fall. And it was as if the monster had gained speed from far below and kept going when it reached the surface of the Lonely Sea. Abaddon flew through the air, arms thrashing and clawing in every direction, until a hundred feet out of the water he latched on to the fourth pillar and began to climb. It was awful to hear the sea monster clang and clamor as it climbed much more swiftly than I'd seen it do before. It was frighteningly fast — like it was holding its breath and needed to move quickly to accomplish its terrible task — and it was gaining on Yipes as he slowly arced up toward the top of the fourth pillar.

"What's going on here?" came a voice from behind us. As if things weren't complicated enough, there stood Jonezy, out of breath from climbing. Anger flashed in his eyes.

"Faster, Yipes! Faster!" I yelled. Jonezy crawled over and saw for himself the scene that was developing before us.

"What have you done, Matilda?" he said.

Abaddon saw that Yipes was moving out of his reach and he moved even faster, the sound of metal on stone filling the still ocean air. And then Abaddon surprised me once more, leaping into the air and coiling into a metal ball covered with razor-sharp corners and jagged steel spikes. The ball spun hideously, spewing boiling black water as it went.

"He's going to make it!" said Jonezy. "He's almost there!"

The three of us watched as the gargantuan metal ball flew straight for Yipes and then unfurled. The arms were out again, reaching for Yipes as they exploded into flames. At the very last possible second, Yipes raised his legs up over his head, pointing his toes into the air and gaining speed. Abaddon flew past, sheering the dangling rope that hung below Yipes. An uncanny, horrible sound wrenched the sea air as Abaddon fell away, crashed into the Lonely Sea, and clawed at the water with furious anger.

I wanted to jump for joy with Matilda and Jonezy, but Yipes's battle wasn't won yet. He was just reaching the top of his flight, and if he missed catching the remains of the rope ladder hanging on the other side, I wasn't sure what we'd do.

"Come on, Yipes. You can do it!" cried Jonezy.

Yipes was a long way off now, but I could see his position well enough to know that it was anyone's guess if he would swing high enough. He was slowing down as he rose, and the wooden rungs and knotted ropes of the old bridge were still at least thirty feet over his head.

"It's going to be close," said Jonezy. "If he swings

back on that vine, it could be a disaster. He might crash into the pillar beneath us."

And just about the time it seemed that Jonezy was right — that Yipes was a tiny bit shy of far enough and was about to come swinging back down — he did something even I didn't think he was crazy enough to do. Yipes swung his legs as far in front of himself as he could and he leaned out from the vine, holding on with just one hand. He swung his legs up and out toward the fourth pillar and managed to catch his foot on one of the old wooden boards of the broken rope bridge. He was carried back toward us by his own settling weight, but the rung of wood held. Yipes was dangling between two worlds, the known world of the third pillar and the unknown of the fourth. He stayed perfectly still a moment, then reached back one hand and took hold of the lowest hanging rope from the old bridge. He tied the swinging rope securely, looked up at us from what was now a lower position on the side of the fourth pillar, and waved.

"Wooooo-hooooo!" I yelled. Matilda and Jonezy celebrated along with me, and we all wished we weren't quite so close to the edge of the third pillar so we could stand up and jump around.

Yipes turned away from us and began to climb up the old bridge. It was very much like a wide wooden ladder strung through with overgrown vines. Climbing to the top was easy work for Yipes, even if it was quite a trek.

When he looked down at us from his perch on the fourth pillar, he waved again.

The rest would be much easier — just like any other skim across a vine — but I was still nervous about sailing over the Lonely Sea with nothing to catch me. While I thought about what it would feel like to be out over the water, Jonezy began to speak.

"I went straight to your cottage this morning, but you were gone. There's something surprising I need to tell you that might help us. It's why I came running after you."

"What is it?" I asked.

"Something Phylo discovered after the night skim."

"Who's Phylo?" I asked.

And then Jonezy shared what he had to tell with Matilda and me.

It was indeed surprising.

CHAPTER 12

A WEAPON
OF OUR OWN

"Let's move away from the edge first, where we can stand up," said Jonezy.

The wind was growing stronger as we crept away from the rim of the third pillar. We would need to walk a good distance to find the beginning of the rope that ran across to where Yipes waited for us. When we were far enough back that I felt safe standing up, I turned toward the inside of the third pillar and looked down inside.

"Someone else is coming," I said, seeing a small figure making their way up the hill. "How is it that everyone seems to know what we're up to?"

Matilda shrugged. We had tried to be secretive about our plans, but it didn't appear to have worked.

"That would be Phylo," said Jonezy. "I told him to wait for my return, but it doesn't surprise me to see him."

It became clear that Phylo was a boy — not very old — and that he was racing up the hill at a steady clip.

"He's strong," I said. "I don't think I could run up the side of the third pillar quite that fast."

"The children are like that," said Matilda. "It must be the fresh sea air and the steady diet of fish and vegetables. It's hard to get them to sleep at night."

"Which is why he was up so late last night, right, Phylo?" asked Jonezy. Phylo had come up beside us, hardly out of breath, and was grinning from ear to ear. He carried a heavy pack over his shoulders.

"Yes, sir!" he said. I looked at Phylo and wondered how old he was. Was he my age or younger? He was slightly taller than me, but there was still the look of a young child in his eyes.

"Can I tell them?" he asked. "I want to tell them!" And this made me think he was no more than ten. The way he'd asked it — as if it were a treasure he could barely contain — had that exuberant quality of the very young.

"You're lucky I don't send you packing back to the village," Jonezy scolded the boy. "I told you to wait for me."

"But it was my idea — I should get to tell," said Phylo. He had enormous eyes and teeth that the rest of his face hadn't grown into yet.

"Oh, just tell us already," said Matilda. "We're right in the middle of something important."

"We'll be getting to that in a moment," said Jonezy, glaring at her. "But first to this discovery of Phylo's." He looked squarely at the boy and folded his arms over his chest. "You may share it."

Phylo hopped up and down excitedly and dropped the pack on the ground with the thudding sound of rocks clanging together.

"After the night skim, I was so awake I couldn't even

imagine trying to sleep. Jonezy always stays with all us boys in a cottage after the night skims. So I waited until he was snoring good and loud and all the other boys were asleep as well. Then I snuck out through the window."

"The mossy surface of the third pillar is so quiet," Jonezy interrupted. "It's not like the House on the Hill or the *Warwick Beacon* where every move is accompanied by a squeaky floorboard. These little urchins are always sneaking around at night. It can't be helped."

Phylo was still smiling and didn't seem to mind being called an urchin.

"I had this idea, see, a great idea!"

"Tell it to me," I said, and Phylo became even more animated.

"I found a nice round rock, the kind I can throw a really long way out into the sea. I carried the rock all the way up here."

Phylo looked around a little bit, then he picked up his pack and ran about twenty feet to the left and a little closer to the rim. He was fearless.

"Right here!" he called back. "This is where I was last night. You see here?"

He kneeled down and began pulling on a piece of moss as we approached.

"Get away from the edge," said Jonezy. "You're too close."

Phylo yanked hard on the moss and fell backward, tumbling down the hill.

"There! I got it!" said Phylo. He stood up and pulled a fat rock from his pack, almost too big to hold.

"The rocks I had last night were just like this one. I smeared them heavy with green."

Phylo turned the moss over and revealed the substance that I had seen the night before. It didn't glow brightly in the daylight. Instead it shimmered and sparkled like a million tiny mirrors in the morning sun. It wasn't powder and it wasn't liquid — it seemed to be both. I remembered touching it and having a hard time getting it off my hands. Phylo spread the green material all over the stone in his hand.

"Where is he?" asked Phylo.

"Where is who?" I asked.

"The monster!"

Matilda and I stared at Phylo and didn't quite know what to make of this boy and his strange ideas.

"Everyone lie down at the edge, where you can see below," said Jonezy. "All but you, Phylo — you stay back."

Phylo nodded and pulled two more hand-sized rocks from his pack. He smeared green on those as well.

When we were all lying down at the edge, we could see that Abaddon was back at the base of the fourth pillar, smashing it with angry arms, pulling chunks of stone free.

"I'm ready when you are," said Phylo.

"Ready for wha —" I said, and looking at Phylo I saw that he'd been busy while my back had been turned. He'd

134

taken two hooked objects from his pack and stabbed them deep into the ground. Across the two hooks ran a length of what appeared to be vine or rope.

"It's a long way — pull it back as hard as you can," said Jonezy. He was pointing directly over our heads toward the sea monster. He turned to me. "Stay low. You don't want to be hit with one of those. He can really fling them."

I glanced back once more and saw that Phylo was a very determined and able boy. He had a pile of five good-sized rocks all covered in green. There was a sixth in his hands, which he had placed inside a sheath of leather at the center of the rope. Then he stretched and stretched until I was sure the rope would snap in half and Phylo would tumble down the hillside. It was a sling like I'd never imagined or seen. I would later discover that very young vines were stretchy in the extreme and could be harvested, but there was no time to ask as I heard the wailing voice of Phylo.

"FIRE!"

The rock sailed over my head with a frightening swish and nearly clobbered me.

"A tiny bit to the right!" said Jonezy.

"And a little higher!" I added, afraid the next one might tag me in the back of the head.

Foooosh! Another rock sailed past.

"To the left now! And farther! Farther!" yelled Jonezy, never taking his eyes off the writhing monster below.

Foooosh! Fooosh! Fooosh!

In rapid succession, three more stones zoomed past my head and out over the water. When the first two finally landed, they hit wide to the left and too short. The two that followed were much closer. One bounced too high, above Abaddon's head, hitting the pillar. The other flew slightly too far right. But the last of them — the fifth stone — hit the pillar and shot into the air. It came down and caught one of Abaddon's twisting arms. And that was when the strangest thing happened.

It stuck. It was as if the glowing green stone had grabbed a hold of Abaddon with claws of its own and would not let go.

"Now wait and see," said Phylo. He had darted up next to me where he sat on his knees. "This is the best part."

We were far enough away that the green stone was nothing more than a speck in the distance on the huge body of the sea monster. And yet, we could see it more plainly the longer we looked.

"It's . . . growing," I stammered.

"Yes, it is!" cried Phylo. He was very proud of himself.

At first Abaddon seemed like a creature annoyed by a fly that had landed on its arm. He swatted at it with another of his long, metallic tentacles. But pretty soon the glowing green had spread across a section that I would have guessed was bigger than me. Abaddon began to scream in a terrible, unearthly voice. His arms burst into flames and he swatted ferociously at the growing green mass.

"That's about it," said Phylo. "Once he bursts into flames, the rock falls off and the green goes away."

And so it did . . . but not right away. It took a little while, and the screaming continued. And it seemed as if Abaddon had to use a lot of energy in order to set himself aflame on the surface of the Lonely Sea.

"It was much better last night," said Phylo. "I brought a big pile of rocks up here, about twenty. I could hear that monster gurgling and chewing away at the stone base of the fourth pillar. I knew where he was, but I couldn't see him, so I launched the first ten stones toward the sound at different speeds. You should see them fly at night! They're like shining green comets. When they hit the water, they sizzle and steam."

"I don't know where he gets these ideas," said Jonezy.

But Phylo was undeterred. I would soon learn that once Phylo started talking, it was difficult to make him stop.

"All those first tries were short, so I shot the rest of what I had harder. And that's when it happened! I hit that thing down there. And BOY did it make him angry. Pretty soon he was bursting into flames and that's when I gathered my things and ran back."

"And then he crept up next to me and shook me awake," said Jonezy. "So he could show me the whole thing all over again."

"An excitable boy," said Matilda.

"If we could keep flinging those green stones at Abaddon," I said, "it might keep him busy. It might even make him want to leave this place."

"That's just what I was thinking!" howled Phylo. "We could rain rocks on him by the thousands!"

I turned to Jonezy and asked, "I wonder what that moss is made of that makes it do all the strange things it does. And why would it attack Abaddon and not us? It's used all the time here on the pillars, but it obviously doesn't agree with Abaddon."

"Actually, there is something you don't know about the moss," said Jonezy. "It has a strong reaction to saltwater."

"So when it hits Abaddon, it also hits all the salty water he's been swimming in," I concluded.

Jonezy nodded. "There's something about the connection between the moss and the saltwater together that makes it unstable. We've always been careful to keep the two away from each other. It helps that the moss only grows on the third pillar, where none of the food is grown and none of the fish are caught."

"It grows on the fourth pillar as well," said Matilda.

The comment bothered Jonezy.

"You don't know that."

"It sure looks like it's covered in moss," said Matilda. "It's green and fuzzy. What else could it be?"

We were still well away from the edge, but the rounded top of the fourth pillar was in plain view. It was bright green, just as the inward curving top of the third pillar we stood on. It was as if the two would fit perfectly together if one were set on top of the other; the green moss would fuse them together like glue. It made me wonder if they had indeed been one taller pillar in a distant past, that one or the other had broken free.

"I can't imagine why or how the moss does what it does," said Matilda. "Only Sir Alistair Wakefield might have known the answer to that."

This logic seemed to quiet Jonezy's concern, if only a little. But I had another, more pressing concern that entered my mind as we stared at the fourth pillar.

"Where's Yipes gone to?" I asked no one in particular. I looked down the long ladder and hoped I wouldn't see him climbing down to take the vine that ran across the Lonely Sea. He wasn't there. He wasn't *anywhere*.

"There's only one way to find out," said Matilda. "It's time to leave."

We looked at each other and smiled, both of us thrilled at the idea of skimming across to an uncharted land.

"You've got that Warvold look in your eye," said Jonezy. "That look always makes me nervous."

"Not to worry," I said. "If there's something over there that can help us, we'll find it and bring it back."

Jonezy looked hard at Matilda.

"You know the sign," he cautioned. "You know what he always said."

"What's he talking about?" I asked Matilda, alarm rising in my voice. "Is Yipes in trouble?"

I gazed across the divide that separated me from my truest friend and wished I could see him.

"It's nothing," said Matilda. But there was a quiver in her voice that made me think otherwise.

"Sir Alistair Wakefield stayed with us a great deal in the beginning," said Jonezy. "He would venture to the fourth pillar only for a day or two, and then he would return. But as time went on and we became more self-sufficient, he stayed away longer. Finally, we came to a point where he visited us only a day here or a night there. The rest of the time he stayed on the fourth pillar, where we were not allowed to go."

"So you're telling me no one ever ventured across that bridge except Sir Alistair Wakefield?"

"That's what I'm telling you."

"There used to be a sign posted on both sides, but it was torn down when the bridge was cut," said Matilda.

"What did the sign say?" I asked, not sure I was ready for the answer.

"I know!" said Phylo. "I remember that sign from before." He'd been obediently quiet all through our conversation, but he really wanted to tell, so Jonezy nodded.

"*The way of yesterday is mine alone. Turn back!* — and it was signed *Sir A. Wakefield.*"

"We have no idea what it meant," Jonezy added, "but we also knew better than to disobey a direct order from

Sir Alistair Wakefield. He asked very little of us, but he really didn't want anyone over there, which is why we've left it alone these long years since his passing."

"I know that place," I said. *"The way of yesterday.* I know what that means."

"What does it mean?" asked Matilda, suddenly very curious.

I didn't know how to explain, but I knew one thing for sure: "If this is anything like the way of yesterday I'm aware of, then we may well find the answers we seek on the other side."

Jonezy hesitated, glancing back and forth between the three of us, trying to be strong in his resolve. But my look crumbled his determination and he nodded quietly. Jonezy didn't bother us with any more questions or concerns, for he knew our minds were made up. As he helped Phylo put his things back in his pack, the two talked about how they would build an army of stone launchers to defeat Abaddon. A moment later, they were walking down the side of the third pillar, busy with their plans, and Matilda asked the question I so longed to hear.

"Are you ready for the ride of your life?"

CHAPTER 13
THE TUBE SLIDE

"You first," said Matilda. "I'll be right behind."

I examined my slider carefully. After the incident at the night skim, I didn't trust the small bit of rope and knots in my hand. It was one thing to fall at the skimming grounds, but quite another if I broke free over the open water with Abaddon awaiting me below.

"You'll never be a great skimmer if you don't learn to trust your slider," Matilda told me. "It won't fail you this time."

Her words rang true. I flipped the slider over the long rope running all the way across to the fourth pillar. A second later, I jumped into the air. Right away, I knew that feeling again — as if I were a bird flying over blue water — and it was fast, faster than any of the skims I'd taken the night before, because it was a steep decline to the other side. The rope arced down at a wide angle and it took my breath away to travel so swiftly. The rope did not provide as smooth a ride as the vines did, and my body shook with tremors all the way down. As I approached the fourth pillar, I crossed the slider in my hands, tightening it around the rope. I was coming in too fast and I cinched the slider tighter still. Heat from the friction began to rise along the rope, and the knots grew hot in my hands.

"Tighter still!" came Matilda's voice behind me. "Feet out front!"

I did as I was told, thrusting my legs forward and crossing the knots as hard as I could. My feet hit the pillar, then my shoulder crashed hard into stone. Matilda came in right behind me, slower and more in control. She steadied us both and helped me get my footing on the wooden rungs of the long hanging ladder.

"Well done," she whispered. "You're fine now. You've done it."

We placed our sliders into our belts and began to climb. It was then that I heard Abaddon below, speaking in his slithery voice of things that would come to pass.

The way of yesterday is not for you. She has brought you to a place you should not have come. But not to worry — she won't be with you much longer!

"You leave her alone!" I screamed.

My whole body was shaking as I felt Matilda lose her footing on the wooden rung where we stood together. It was unlike her, but she quickly recovered and we stood firm on the rung once more. She shook her head as if to wake all her senses and stay alert.

"Who are you talking to, Alexa?" she asked.

How could I possibly explain all that had happened to me? How once I could hear the voice of Elyon and now

I heard that of Abaddon — the voices of good and evil in the world?

"Let's get to the top and find Yipes," I said. "I don't want him to be without us any longer."

Matilda nodded weakly, then untied the rope leading back to the third pillar and tucked it firmly into her belt. She passed to the side of me and we moved on, Matilda in front, me following close behind. It was a lot farther than I realized. Things always look so small from a distance, but there were at least a hundred rungs on the fallen bridge. Some were broken or weakened so that each step had to be carefully taken.

"Yipes did this so fast," Matilda said as she tugged softly on a board to check its sturdiness. "How does he do things like that?"

"He probably used the vines on the sides and didn't bother with the rungs," I said. "He's not like us — I mean, he's got certain talents that are hard to explain."

Matilda looked up the long distance we had left to go. "So I see."

It was another ten minutes before we reached the very top and felt the soft, furry face of the fourth pillar. The moss here was even brighter and spongier than that of the third pillar. I was immediately concerned about the terrain.

"This is steeper than it looked," I said. There was barely a place to stand on the rim of the fourth pillar — maybe a foot of relatively flat moss, two at the most — and then the squishy landscape rose fast and high.

144

Matilda had crouched down and was pulling on the edge of a flat wooden corner sticking out of the moss. As she tugged, a soft, wet sound filled the air. The wood slid free of the moss and popped out. It was a sign.

"The bridge to yesterday is mine alone. Turn back," I read aloud.

"We have to stop thinking that way," said Matilda. She picked up the sign and flung it over the edge, where it bobbed and flipped out of sight toward the water below. She pulled the long, heavy rope from her belt and tied it tightly to one of the posts where the rope bridge had been anchored.

"It's about time!" came a voice from well above us. "I was beginning to wonder if I'd have to cross back over and come looking for you."

"Yipes!" Matilda and I both cried at the same moment. We were so very happy to see him. He scampered down the side of the fourth pillar faster than I thought was a good idea.

"Slow down! You're scaring me!" I said, afraid he'd keep right on running off the end as he gained speed.

"Not to worry," he shouted, digging his heels in as he approached, then coming to a stop a few feet above without any trouble. He was grinning broadly as he pulled both of us up the hill toward the top. "I've found something interesting. You're not going to believe it when you see it. Come on, up this way!"

Yipes wouldn't tell us what it was, and he seemed

especially uncertain about how I would react. He showed us how to dig our feet into the moss and make good traction, so we wouldn't slide down. As we went, I was amazed by the simplicity of the fourth pillar. There was nothing but cool green against a blue sky. And it was perfectly shaped on every side I could see, like the furry soft head of a very tall giant.

After a while, the slope of the hill we climbed became less fierce. It leveled off near the top and then became entirely flat when we reached the summit.

"There's a lot more flat space than appears from the other side," said Matilda, catching her breath. She was exuberant with curiosity, which was exactly how I felt.

I loved that we saw this moment the same way.

"Everything seems so far away from here," I said. "Like we're standing alone above the whole world."

"But there's always somewhere higher to climb," said Yipes. He looked over his shoulder and we followed his gaze. It was true I was higher than I'd ever been within the realm of the Five Stone Pillars, but the fifth pillar stood so much grander still. The first, second, and third pillars were below me now and I could see them clearly, but the top of the fifth pillar with its jagged wall of sharp stone remained an imposing facade above me.

"Somehow I don't think we'll be visiting there anytime soon," I said.

"Look there," said Yipes, pointing to the side of the

fourth stone pillar hidden from view if you stood on pillar one, two, or three.

What I saw creeping into view was not at all welcome.

"That thing can't be trusted," I said. "You of all people should know better."

I glanced at Yipes, then back at the small animal that was advancing carefully in our direction. It was entirely black with sharp yellow eyes that stared me down as if to ask me why I'd come here. It had the shape and liquid slow movement of something I'd seen long before in the Bridewell library.

"Not all cats are alike," said Yipes. For that's just what it was — a black cat slinking quietly toward us.

"What do you have against cats?" asked Matilda, taken aback at my reaction.

"They're bad," I said. And I meant it. Sam and Pepper, the only two cats I had ever known, had been as dreadful as any two animals could be. They had betrayed everyone.

"Don't mind her," said Yipes. "She has a complicated history with cats."

"It wants us to follow it," said Matilda. She was already moving across the top of the stone pillar. I took hold of her hand and pulled her back.

"I don't think this is a good idea."

"Well, I'm going," said Yipes. "I trust this particular feline, at least enough to follow it a little while. I think it wants to show us something on the other side."

147

"What if it's trying to trick us?" I asked. "There could be slippery rocks over there. There could be a monster or a trap."

"I'm going," repeated Yipes. He took one step forward, but I had cast a shadow of doubt over him and he stopped short.

"Will you come with me?" he asked Matilda. "We can leave Alexa here to bake in the sun."

I scowled at Yipes, but I was beginning to see that we didn't have a lot of choices. From what we'd seen, there was nothing else on the fourth pillar to help us.

"All right, I'll go," I said. "But let's take it slow. I still don't trust that thing."

Yipes led out and we made our way across the flat top of the fourth pillar. The black cat advanced and stayed well ahead of us as we followed, until it disappeared down the sloping side.

"I told you!" I said. "It wants to draw us down the side, to send us slipping and sliding off the edge. This is crazy!"

"We don't know for sure," said Matilda. This was a reckless side of her I hadn't seen before. "Let's go just a little farther and look down. Maybe the cat is standing there waiting for us."

"Abaddon has used cats before," I said. "They're the only animal I know besides hawks that have sided with him. Yipes — tell her."

But Yipes wouldn't banish an entire species because of two misguided library cats.

"There are a few bad people in the world as well, but that doesn't mean we're all doomed to the same fate. Give this a chance, Alexa. I have a feeling about it."

I could not stop thinking it was a bad idea, but I also had to admit that there was truth in what Yipes was saying. So the three of us walked the last twenty feet to the end of the flat plain of the fourth pillar. It sloped down sharply on the other side — faster than on the side we'd come from.

"Where'd it go?" asked Yipes. The cat had disappeared. "Here, kitty, kitty, kitty."

"I don't think that's going to work," I said. "It's found some way to hide so we'll go down there looking for it."

I was feeling vindicated, but then something happened that was so unexpected I almost slid right down the mossy green hill leading to the sea.

The cat meowed. It spoke something in its own language from a hidden place I could not see. I heard the voice of this creature. And I *understood* what it was saying.

"Over here, this way!" meowed the cat.

"Please tell me you heard that," I asked Yipes and Matilda.

Matilda was awestruck. "It's some sort of trick of magic from that monster below."

149

Yipes was backing up, and I could tell by the wide circles of his eyes that he'd heard the cat as well. The command came once more.

"This way! Hurry!" meowed the cat.

"It's been too long since I've heard a voice like that," Yipes said breathlessly. He was astonished, but happy, like a great memory from childhood had swept over him. "I'd forgotten how it sounds — exactly like a cat, only I understand it."

The idea seemed to enchant Yipes, and yet the cat's words had concerned him.

"Maybe you were right," he said. "Maybe this *is* an evil cat."

And then, as if to answer Yipes's concern, the cat spoke again.

"You and your friends are welcome here, Alexa Daley. This way!"

Matilda made a little yelping sound of surprise and hopped backward.

"That thing knows who you are!" she said. "How can that be?"

"I don't know," I said. "But I'm starting to think we should find out."

"That's right," meowed the cat. "This way!"

"It can talk *and* it's invisible!" said Yipes. He sounded more certain than ever that we were dealing with something dangerous. "Don't go down there!"

But it was too late — I'd already made up my mind. I

don't know if it was my immense curiosity or if I'd begun to trust the sound of this cat's voice, but something told me to make my way down the side of the fourth pillar. Matilda wasn't about to let me go alone, and she quickly came up beside me.

"Wait for me!" cried Yipes.

We didn't have very far to go until we all realized at once that the side of the fourth pillar we were on wasn't exactly what it seemed. The color of green here wasn't all one shade. It varied in places from light to slightly darker and back again, and as we crept down the side and neared a patch of darker green, we understood why this was true. There were wide, oddly shaped openings in the ground. Along the sides of the openings, the moss ran every bit as thick as it did on the top of the fourth pillar. From somewhere inside, there was light shining through.

"How is that possible?" asked Yipes, voicing what we were all thinking. Somehow there was light *inside* the fourth pillar, softly illuminating the sides of the wide holes. The light played with shadow and made it seem as if there weren't any openings at all, only different shades of green on a singular surface.

"Follow me!" The meow returned, only this time the sound echoed softly. It was coming from deep inside the hole directly in front of us. All three of us crept near the edge of the hole and looked down. It was very steep and shaped like a tube. It turned after a few feet in a way that made it impossible to see where it went.

"Come on then — in you go!" said the cat.

"We're not going in there," said Yipes, fiddling nervously with his long mustache. We were still leaning over and looking into the hole. This had a lot to do with what happened next. It began with a terrible shrieking noise from directly behind us. Matilda screamed and jumped from the terrible sound behind her, and when she turned, she lost her balance and fell down the hole with a *thwoooop!* Yipes waited for exactly zero seconds before jumping in after her, and this left me balancing precariously between a giant hole in the ground and something hissing at me from behind.

"You shouldn't make Nimbus wait for you," said the feline voice behind me. "It's hard enough getting her out at all when there are no clouds in the sky."

I turned in the direction of the voice and found that the terrifying sound we'd heard had come from a smaller than average cat. She was black as spilled ink with dazzling yellow eyes — just like the cat we'd seen — but this one appeared to be longer and as skinny as a rail.

"Don't make me push you," meowed the cat. She was one of those kinds of animals that has no idea how small they are.

I turned and yelled down the hole for Yipes and Matilda, but there was no answer. It was a mistake to turn my back on a cat at the edge of a deep hole. Before I could turn around, the little monster had jumped on my leg and was digging her claws into my skin.

"Owwwwwww!" I yelled. And then I, too, fell into the hole.

Once I stopped tumbling and settled in for the ride, it was slick. I swished and slid as the tube twisted and turned on the way down. The long, skinny black cat jumped free of my leg and I lost sight of her. A little farther down, I zoomed past the first cat, who held firm against one of the high walls of the tube and watched me slide by. I looked over my head as I kept going and saw the skinny cat come alongside its companion. The two appeared to be laughing.

I hate cats.

There was a long, straight shot toward the bottom of the tube that slowly leveled off. By the time I came to the very end, I was barely moving.

When I finally stopped, I found that I could not get up. This was not because of any injury I'd sustained on the way down. If anything, I'd just enjoyed one of the more thrilling rides of my life and shouldn't have minded getting up. I couldn't move because I was paralyzed with disbelief at what lay before my eyes.

And now I shall venture to describe all that I saw as two black cats slinked past me without a word between them.

CHAPTER 14

THE PİLLAR OF YESTERDAY

"How can this be?" I stammered, trying to understand the vast improbability of what I saw. It felt like I'd stumbled upon an elaborate carnival or a strange circus halfway between setup and teardown.

I stood up and took in a deep breath of sea air, for there was plenty to be had. I faced a vast opening in the side of the fourth pillar that spanned hundreds of feet across and up into the air. Light poured into an equally immense space within the fourth pillar, and standing high and tall in the very center of the room was the biggest balloon I'd ever seen. It was shaped like an ice-cream cone — round on top and narrow at the bottom — and it was attached by vines to a big box that seemed to anchor the balloon to the ground. There were rudders at the back of the box and what looked like vast wings along its side.

The ceiling of the chamber or cave — I couldn't figure out what to call the place I'd arrived in — was much higher still than the top of the balloon. All along the wall to my left were living creatures of the sea. And I could see them all, because they were encased in clear boxes that defied imagination. Gigantic, long panes of glass separated me from fish and sea creatures of every size and color, many of which I'd never seen before.

And there was more — so much more — as I walked toward my friends, who stood gazing in a different direction.

"What is this place?" I said as I came alongside. We were all staring together now, and it appeared that my companions were not able to answer me, for they didn't speak at all. There was a towering replica of the Wakefield House rising all the way to the ceiling, hundreds of feet above. I gasped at the sight of it, for it brought Roland and Thomas and their incredible journey into such clear focus. The model looked as if it might topple over at any moment — just like in their story — and I marveled at its warped genius. Who could have made such a thing as this? Who could have even thought to *try* to make it?

Rows of stairs and landings and tables crisscrossed all around the model of the Wakefield House and up into the air. The landings wound through, across bridges that connected to yet more landings surrounding parts of the giant balloon. This vast series of landings ran all through the ceiling of the chamber in twisting, turning levels of high and low. It was impossibly complex and, just like the Wakefield House, it looked as if it might all come tumbling down at any moment.

Alongside the Wakefield House was yet another

model, this one of all five stone pillars standing in a circle, rising high into the chamber where I couldn't see their tops. There were long, teetering ladders that had been leaned precariously against them all.

"He will be surprised to see you."

The words came from a voice I had never heard before. It was so very slowly said, like an ancient voice, grumbling and papery, bothered by having to speak at all and having to work very hard to do it.

"Who said that?" asked Matilda. We all looked in the direction of the voice — up and to the right on one of the many landings. Leaning over and looking down toward us was a mammoth lizard, its tongue darting slowly in and out. By the size of its deep green head, I would have guessed it was more than ten feet long.

"That's a very long tongue you've got there," said Yipes. He giggled nervously and I slapped him in the arm.

"I don't think we should be talking to that thing," I said. "We don't know anything about it."

The skinnier of the two black cats crept into sight and stood right on top of the giant lizard's head. The other cat — the fatter one called Nimbus — also emerged from the side. The lizard began creeping across the landing and its full body came into view. It was even bigger than I'd thought.

"Do you think he's coming down to eat us?" Yipes asked.

I heard a sound from somewhere far above, and the words of the giant lizard returned in my mind.

He will be surprised to see you.

I turned my gaze from the approaching lizard to the ceiling. To my utter astonishment, there was someone at the top of the tallest ladder, the one that leaned against the fifth pillar with its jagged rock walls. And this someone was coming down toward us.

I poked Matilda in the shoulder and pointed up. We both looked on in silence, wondering and waiting.

"Do you think it could be . . ." Matilda started to ask, but Yipes cut her off.

"That thing is getting *really* close."

The lizard was stealthier than it looked. It had climbed all the way down a wood pole and was advancing toward us in long strides. Both cats had climbed on its back for the ride. The long tongue of the lizard zipped in and out. As it came within a few feet, we began to huddle together and move back as a group.

"I told you we shouldn't trust those cats," I said. "Look what they've gotten us into!"

We were about to turn and run as a group when there came a voice from above.

"Don't mind Grump. He's harmless."

It was another ancient voice — slow and choppy. The man had come to the bottom of the ladder and turned to us. He shuffled silently in our direction and I saw that he was indeed very old, older than I thought anyone could be. His beard was tucked under itself, like he was trying to protect the flowing white strands at the end and wanted to keep them hidden. His face looked tougher or somehow harder than a face was allowed to be. It had the solid appearance of stone — a face showing its long past when it ought to have been buried in the ground already. How many hundreds of years old was he? If I was guessing his identity correctly and Roland's story was to believed, he was at least three hundred, maybe four hundred, years old. And yet his cheeks were still flush with color, his blue eyes still darting back and forth with excitement at the sight of visitors.

"You have come to the pillar of yesterday," said the man.

"Sir Alistair Wakefield?" I asked, for it could be no other that stood before us. "But you're . . . you're *dead*."

The old man seemed to wonder about this idea for a moment, as if the thought of being dead or alive had long been beside the point.

He patted his own chest and shoulders with a boney hand, and rightfully replied, "Nope. Still here."

"But . . ." I began.

"You of all people should know, Alexa Daley. Sometimes old people only seem dead to everyone else, but they're very much alive."

I was more than a little surprised to find that he knew

my name, and I was about to ask him about it when Matilda broke in.

"But everyone *thinks* you're dead," she said, clearly astonished by this turn of events.

"Fewer distractions that way," said Sir Alistair. "I've had a lot of work to do."

Yipes glanced around the space. "I'll say you have!"

Sir Alistair seemed very interested in Yipes upon hearing his voice. He turned his gaze on my friend and hobbled a few steps toward him.

"I've heard about you," he said. He held out his thin hand and Yipes shook it vigorously.

"Calm down, Yipes," I said. "You're going to hurt him."

"Not to worry. I haven't had a good, hard shake in a long time. It feels magnificent!" said Sir Alistair.

Yipes took this to heart and began shaking poor Sir Alistair's hand even harder until Matilda tapped him on the shoulder.

"I think that's probably enough," she said softly.

Yipes let go and Sir Alistair, relieved at being let go, turned his attention squarely on me.

"I see you've already met Nimbus and Midnight," he said. "And I imagine you're a little surprised to understand what they're saying."

I looked at the two cats and thought about this a moment.

"Are you the only one to ever come here, to the fourth pillar?" I asked.

"That I am," he answered. "Roland has come around below on the *Warwick Beacon* and brought me things in a way that we have devised, but it has been only I, no one else."

"Then I'm not surprised," I said matter-of-factly. "People kill magic, and there has been only you, so the magic remains on the fourth pillar. It's a wild place."

"But now you've arrived, and I'm glad of it!" said Sir Alistair. "The time for this place to drift away has come. Let the magic fade if it must. Surely it will remain somewhere, in places we can't find."

I felt a concern that I hadn't voiced at hearing Sir Alistair speak of Roland so casually, as if he were still alive.

"You know about our difficulties getting here, about Abaddon and the *Warwick Beacon*," I said.

Sir Alistair Wakefield went silent and tucked the loose strands at the bottom of his silvery beard with slender fingers.

"He knows," meowed Midnight. "Nimbus and I saw everything, then we came back here. It was not a good day on the fourth pillar."

"I've stayed on far too long," said Sir Alistair, his voice melancholy. "Many are waiting for me at the very end of the road, and yet I remain in the world year after long year, toiling alone."

"Does the road you speak of lead to the Tenth City?" I asked, certain that it did. He nodded, piercing me with his blue eyes at the thought of going home.

"We're here now," said Yipes. "To keep you company."

"And to ask for your help," said Matilda. She was the only one among us that hadn't lost sight of our purpose.

Sir Alistair Wakefield stood tall and seemed to have moved past his own self-pity.

"It's time we turned our gaze in another direction," he said, looking toward the massive opening to the outside. "To the monster that must be defeated."

CHAPTER 15

FALLING PILLARS
OF STONE

"Why do you have a giant lizard?" asked Matilda. We had moved to a table that looked out into the sea and we were enjoying fresh bread and cooked fish. Sir Alistair had a passable kitchen on the fourth pillar, the center-piece of which was an imposing stone oven for baking, which, he claimed, was always cooking something. Next to the oven were complicated devices for dropping and raising nets in and out of the Lonely Sea.

"Grump," said Sir Alistair, "is very good company. He hardly ever talks, which makes him a good compan-ion, given that I talk all the time. Although sometimes it's difficult to tell whether or not he's actually paying any attention to me."

"Where did he come from?"

Sir Alistair looked at Grump, who was staring at us with lazy eyes. I couldn't say for sure if he was awake or asleep.

"Roland found him somewhere out there," said Sir Alistair, nodding toward the Lonely Sea. "Grump was a lot smaller when he showed up twenty or so years ago."

"So there are other places on the Lonely Sea besides The Land of Elyon and the Five Stone Pillars?"

"Not that I've seen. But according to Roland, there are a few."

I instantly wanted to know more about where Grump had come from and what else could be found there. I made a mental note to ask Grump if he could remember from which direction he'd come.

"And the cats?" asked Yipes. "What about Nimbus and Midnight? Why are they here?"

Midnight was sitting on the corner of the table, licking her paw, and Nimbus was curled up next to Grump.

"Two girls looking for adventure," meowed Midnight.

"Speak for yourself," Nimbus meowed.

"The last time Roland pulled up to the bottom of the pillar with things I'd asked for, there was a wooden box among the supplies." Sir Alistair explained. "These two were inside. I think he might have thought I could use a companion or two." He stroked Midnight's black coat and the cat purred thankfully. "They've got a fascinating story of their own, as we all do. Two curious cats that stowaway in other people's things and end up on a very long trip."

I still didn't trust Nimbus and Midnight. I didn't like the way they'd tricked us or the way they looked at me now. But it was so refreshing to hear them talking. I *loved* hearing them talk.

"How much longer do you think it will last?" I asked, knowing full well that the fourth stone pillar was now crawling with humans and the magic of talking to animals was likely to waver and burn out.

163

"You mean understanding them? Hard to say," said Sir Alistair with an air of concern. "But I think our time on the fourth pillar is coming to an end anyway."

As if to make his point, we all heard Abaddon below, enraged and slamming his monstrous tentacles into stone. Yipes looked to Sir Alistair with some concern.

"Why is he doing that? Why doesn't he just climb to the top?"

"Because it's too far, even for him. Those tentacles of metal and bone can only carry the awful weight of him so high. I believe it's part of Elyon's plan that this is so. Abaddon can't climb high enough to reach the top of any of the pillars, so you can guess what he must be thinking."

"That he can knock them down!" cried Yipes. He was thrilled at having discovered the answer and stood right up when he said it.

"That's right," said Sir Alistair. "And the fourth stone pillar — this pillar we sit on — is the thinnest of them all." He looked directly at Yipes, who had just then stuffed a very large bite of bread into his mouth to reward himself. "And why do you suppose he's trying to knock it down?"

Yipes tried to answer, but we couldn't understand him.

"I like Yipes," meowed Nimbus. "He's amusing."

"Wait," said Matilda. "I know why. He's only banging away at the pillar on the one side, the side that faces the third pillar, where we do all the skimming. He wants to knock more than just the one down. He wants to send them all falling down, one on top of the other."

"If he can't have them for himself, he'll destroy them trying," I mumbled.

"That's probably true," began Sir Alistair. "But I don't think it's the whole truth. I believe he thinks toppling the fourth pillar will do one of two things. Either it will bring one crashing into another and leave it at an angle that he can climb, or one will break in half and leave a short enough distance for him to climb. One way or another, he wants out of the Lonely Sea."

"Sir Alistair," I said timidly. I had a question I'd wanted to ask but wasn't sure he would answer. It was a question that pertained to the things we were speaking of in an especially important way. "Did you make the Five Stone Pillars as you made the Wakefield House?"

"You know all about the Wakefield House, do you?"

I nodded that I did. It was one of the places I'd liked hearing about most when Roland told the story of his childhood. The Wakefield House had been like one of the Five Stone Pillars, only it was much more fragile and primitive in its design. Once a pile of stone rising high into the sky with hidden mazes inside, it had collapsed — served its purpose, Roland had said — after its secrets had been discovered.

"I'm afraid that was a little bit different than the Five

Stone Pillars. I can't say that I made this place. I found it. Although all of this in here — this is all of my own making." He waved his arm across the room to indicate everything that was in the chamber.

"What's it all for?" I asked. "All these strange things you're doing don't seem to make any sense."

At these words, Sir Alistair became more serious.

"This was all for the moment we find ourselves in right now, Alexa Daley. I've been alive longer than anyone — hundreds of years. Generation after generation has passed, and yet here I am. And sometimes — though not for a very long time — Elyon has spoken to me. He has guided my hands in ways I don't always understand, ways that people of this world would scoff at. But there is a purpose for all that I have made, even if I don't understand for certain what that purpose is."

I looked all about the room once more and had a very hard time imagining what this place could have to do with defeating Abaddon.

"How is it that you're still alive at all? You've left the way of yesterday behind, and yet you still live."

"My, you do know a lot about me!" said Sir Alistair, laughing gracefully. "Roland was a very quiet man most of the time, but if you got him talking he would say a lot, wouldn't he? He told me all about you just as he told you about me. I guess a sailor has to talk sometime."

I was a little embarrassed to think of what Roland

would have said about *me*. Especially since he hadn't been here for years.

"To answer your question — and bear in mind that this is only a guess — I think I'm aging at about half the pace as I'm meant to. I spent hundreds of years past the way of yesterday, and my clock is still running a little slower than it should. But even I can't last forever."

I looked around the immense cavern and had so many questions. My eyes lit on the giant balloon and I found I couldn't take my eyes off of it.

"That's for you," said Sir Alistair. "It's my crowning achievement, you might say."

"For *me*?" I asked. It was frightening to think what he'd want me to do with a balloon that big. What was it even for?

Nimbus perked up from where she lay resting at Grump's side, her ears pointing toward the tunnel where we'd entered.

"Someone's coming," she purred.

"Who could it be?" Matilda asked. "You don't think Phylo would have tried to follow us here?"

I could think of no one else besides Jonezy who even knew we'd come across. Maybe it was him with news to report.

Grump slithered across the floor of the chamber toward the tunnel, his thick tail swishing back and forth as he moved. He arrived at the opening at just about the same moment the intruder found his way to the bottom.

"Can someone please tell this monster to back away from me?" the intruder asked.

It was a voice I neither expected nor wanted to hear. Marco, the one individual on the Five Stone Pillars I trusted even less than Nimbus and Midnight, had arrived on the fourth pillar.

CHAPTER 16

OF MOSS AND SALTWATER

"Go ahead, Grump," Yipes said as we came up alongside Marco. "You can eat this one."

Grump's tongue darted out and almost touched Marco on the knee, which made him jump for the tube and try to escape.

"It's too steep and slippery," meowed Midnight. "You can't get out by that way."

Marco jumped free of the tube and moved in front of the row of towering fish tanks.

"What kind of crazy place is this?" he said, hitting the sides of his head and wondering how it was that he could understand the voice of a cat.

A shark the same size as Grump had moved in behind Marco in one of the tanks, staring at him from behind the glass.

"You shouldn't have come here," I said. And then, turning to Nimbus and Midnight, I asked, "Where's the way out so we can send him back?"

Marco had swung around and was backing slowly away from the tank and the shark within.

"Yes . . . by any means. Show me the way out of here!"

"Not so fast!" said Sir Alistair. He was at the balloon, checking the ropes that were tied to the giant box on the floor. "You look like a strong young man."

"Sir Alistair Wakefield?" said Marco. "But — but you're dead!"

Sir Alistair shuffled up next to Marco and placed a hand on his shoulder. "Just about the time it seems a man's work is done and the world has used him up, he may find himself needed the most."

"What's that supposed to mean?" Marco asked, gazing at all the oddities in the chamber.

"It means I'm not dead after all. And I need your help."

After a flurry of questions about talking animals and the many strange attractions within the fourth stone pillar, Marco finally calmed down enough to consider making himself useful.

"I don't trust him one bit," I said. Between Marco and the cats, I was really starting to sound paranoid. But what could I do?

"It's all of us against the one monster, and even then our chances are slim," Matilda said to me. "You're going to have to learn to trust him." She looked at Midnight and Nimbus, who seemed to be taking a nap. "*And* them."

I started to protest, but quickly realized she was right. There was no time for arguing as Abaddon continued to pound away at the pillar.

There was a quiet trembling under my feet, and the balloon rocked gently back and forth.

"The tower is weakening," said Sir Alistair. He waved us all to a long table strewn with papers and instruments. One of the gadgets on the table appeared to be some sort of measuring device. There were globs of colored balls inside an oblong, clear box. The box was filled with thick liquid and the balls floated free.

"As I suspected," said Sir Alistair. "We're not as perfectly level as we once were."

"Uh-oh," said Yipes. "That can't be good."

"You mean the fourth pillar has moved?" I asked.

"That's exactly it," Sir Alistair answered with concern. "We may only have days, even hours before he has his way."

We all stood in silence trying to wrap our brains around the idea that very soon the world of the Five Stone Pillars might come to an end.

"What do you need me to do?" asked Marco. I still didn't think he could be trusted, but at least he was willing to help.

Sir Alistair directed us to follow him to the box beneath the balloon.

"I've been at this for years and years, trying to perfect it," he said. "This is a flying machine and flying is a complicated business."

"Flying?" I said. "You mean this thing is meant to go

171

out there?" I looked out through the vast opening to the blue sky with puffy white clouds.

"Of course it is," said Marco. "What else would he do with it?"

I glared at him. Why did he have to be such a know-it-all?

"I had hoped for a long time to speak with the sea-birds and build something different, something more like them. But I could never break through. Land animals — things like cats and giant lizards — are, for reasons I can't figure out, easier to converse with." He looked at the long bank of fish tanks. "I can't get a word out of them, either."

Marco was running his hand along the box. It was twenty or more feet in diameter, but it was only about five feet high. He ran his hands along the worn rail of the box and lifted himself inside.

"Lots of room in here," he said. "What's that?"

I gave Yipes a little boost, and he was perched up on the ledge in an instant, gazing inside. Matilda and I grabbed the rail and pulled ourselves up, leaning over the edge of the box and looking in. We saw that it was complicated and vast inside. There were rows of benches along two sides, and beneath the benches hung rows of hammocks in the darkened recesses. There were levers and pulleys, boxes and shelves — and it all had the familiar Sir Alistair Wakefield craziness about it, as if it might just fall apart at the very moment of liftoff. In the center, there was a round tube of glass surrounded at its base by a square box. The glass tube ran twice as high as the box and pointed straight up into the balloon.

"Don't touch that," said Sir Alistair, seeing that Marco was reaching out for it. "It's hot."

Sir Alistair explained that he'd tried a great many ways of generating heated air, all of which had failed to provide the result he was looking for.

"I could get it filled and moving, but then the hot air would run out and the balloon would sink to one side. It wasn't until very recently that I discovered a way. And it was hidden under my nose all along."

"The moss," said Matilda. Right when she said it, I thought the same thing. Phylo had figured it out.

Sir Alistair was momentarily crestfallen to find that his discovery was already known, but he quickly rebounded and went on.

"Why, yes, the moss! I'd known that it did strange things when combined with saltwater, but for some reason it never occurred to me to put that idea to use when it came to the balloon. It was he who told me."

Sir Alistair looked down at Grump, and the hulking beast spoke for the first time in quite a while in his sleepy-sounding voice.

"He can be tiresome when he fails for a long time without a breakthrough."

Sir Alistair knelt down and tapped Grump's back softly with a look of understanding.

. "As I said, he's a good listener. I imagine he heard me rant and rave for years about this balloon before helping me come to my senses."

"So the balloon is full of hot air right now?" I asked.

"It has been for the past few weeks. It's only sitting there because I've got it tied down."

There were great vines tied to pins embedded in the floor of the chamber on four sides. Sir Alistair slid a door along the side of the box beneath the balloon and stepped inside, guiding us all in with him. He opened the lid to a box and poked inside with a long, sharp stick. When the stick emerged, it held a chunk of moss.

"The bottom of the tube is filled with about a foot of saltwater from the Lonely Sea. And when I drop this in . . ."

Sir Alistair raised his arm and held the moss over the opening of the tube, scraping it off the stick. It fell with a plop and a loud hissing sound. The tube filled with white fog that became thicker and thicker.

"Then all you have to do is turn the crank," said Sir Alistair.

"Let me!" said Yipes. He grabbed hold of two handles that poked out of the floor of the box we stood in. The handles were high enough off the base of the box that Yipes had some trouble getting a hold on them. But he was able to get them going, pulling on one and then the other, until a soft, whirling sound could be heard from beneath the tube.

"You see there," said Sir Alistair, pointing to the tube. "The heat that comes off the moss is immense when it hits the saltwater — it doesn't take much when it's mixed with the air already in the balloon."

The misty white inside the tube rushed up, expanding the balloon, and we could all feel the big box trying to lift off the ground. If not for the vines that held it, we would have crashed into the ceiling.

"That's magnificent!" said Yipes. "Let's fly it right now!"

Sir Alistair had to gently pull Yipes away from the handles for fear of pushing too much heat into the balloon and breaking the vines.

"That little bit of moss will continue to smolder for hours. And it will flame up, like a bright coal on a fire, whenever we add air from underneath. But we can't fly it yet."

"Why not?" asked Yipes, genuinely disappointed.

"Because it's never been flown. No one has ever seen it — including Abaddon — and we don't want him seeing what we're up to. We'll have to wait until after nightfall."

Sir Alistair produced a set of maps and charts from an alcove and laid them out on the wide ledge of the box. There were wooden pins on the edge and he pulled them out, moved the pile of charts into position, and sent the wooden pins through holes in the paper. I could see how this might be done when the balloon was flying in order to keep the papers from flying away.

"Roland helped a great deal with these," said Sir Alistair.

"They do look familiar," said Yipes. He had hopped right up on the ledge of the box and was leaning over, looking at one of the maps.

"Traveling by air is very like much the same as traveling by sea," said Sir Alistair. "I've been using the same methods to chart a course, and weather patterns are equally tantamount. The wings and the rudders can be used to force the balloon one way or another for a time, but on long journeys, the balloon will be forced to go where the wind will carry it. See here, where this list of arrows and days are?"

We all nodded.

"There are times during the yearly cycle when the prevailing winds will carry you one way or another. These winds cycle through every few months in this series of oval patterns, and they are highly predictable."

I had wondered silently what the point of all this was from the moment Sir Alistair began speaking of the balloon and what it would do. Why fly at all — what would be the point? Looking at one of the maps, and seeing The Land of Elyon plainly in the distance from the Five Stone Pillars, I finally put two and two together.

"This is a way home, a way back to The Land of Elyon." But then, just as quickly as I'd said it, I wondered aloud how many people the flying craft would hold.

"About a dozen adults or twice as many children," said

Sir Alistair. We all looked at him like we couldn't believe it, and he responded by telling us the balloon was huge — with 600,000 cubic feet of capacity. Then he started going into a lot of scientific facts about things like grams of heated and cooled air. We all glazed over, completely lost, and he simply said, "Trust me. It will hold a lot of weight."

We were all more than happy to agree.

"And the time comes nearer than you might have imagined. We are right now at precisely the right moment to be flying away from the Five Stone Pillars in the direction of The Land of Elyon. A trip could be made anytime in the next few weeks and the wind will hold."

The thought of it was mesmerizing. Drifting over the Lonely Sea on a giant flying machine, arriving to the astonishment of my parents and everyone else in Lathbury. It would be amazing!

"I want to fly it," I said.

Again Sir Alistair spoke as much with his piercing eyes as he did his papery voice.

"Then fly it you shall."

A tingle of excitement ran through me.

"Where's Marco?" asked Matilda. He had disappeared while we were immersed in the charts.

"Right here," he said, popping out from behind the other side of the box and startling all of us. "Just looking at the way this thing is held together. Very ingenious."

"Stop snooping around," I said, and even I thought it sounded a little bit too mistrustful.

"Hey — I'm just trying to understand this contraption. It's not the sort of thing a person sees every day."

"How about I put you to work on something more pressing at the moment?" said Sir Alistair. He looked at Yipes. "In fact, you could both work together, up top. I need moss. *Lots* of moss, and it's not the simplest thing for an old man like me to get hold of."

"As long as he promises not to push me down the hill," said Yipes. "He's got a reputation for mischief."

Marco grimaced and shook his head. "I'll admit I don't much like having you and Alexa around. I don't like the idea of being forced to leave this place. But I'm not trying to get rid of you."

Yipes glanced at me. We knew each other's secret looks as though they were a language all their own. Neither of us was convinced. As far as we were concerned, Marco was guilty until proven innocent and had to be watched carefully. The thought of Yipes and Marco working together made me nervous.

"And you, Alexa," continued Sir Alistair. "You're going to have to go back and tell everyone what we're doing. If you leave now, you can return before nightfall and we'll do a test flight. Matilda will help me prepare the balloon in your absence."

"I'm not sure . . ." said Matilda. I could see that Matilda didn't like the idea of sending me off on my own. But she was soon convinced that we all needed to do our

178

part, and only one of us could be spared to travel back to the third pillar.

I knew something she didn't. I knew that the people would listen if Jonezy told them the truth about me. Some may not want to go along — and the truth was we couldn't fit them all at once even if the balloon worked — but at least they would listen.

"Time is running short," said Sir Alistair. "We better hurry."

Matilda put her arm around me and pulled me close. "Be careful going across," she whispered.

I paused and looked about the room at all the strange and wonderful inventions of Sir Alistair Wakefield.

"This place is worth saving. We have to find a way."

CHAPTER 17

EXPOSING AN HEIR TO THE THRONE

I stood at the edge of the fourth pillar holding the rope. Marco was still at the top, picking moss and placing it into a big wooden bucket, but Yipes had come with me.

"I'll move the rope back down right after you're safely across."

"Thank you, Yipes. Thank you for everything. I couldn't do any of this without you."

"Soon we'll be flying," he said. "*Really* flying! Maybe even toward home. Just get back here as fast as you can and make good use of your time. They'll listen to you. You can be very persuasive when you want to be."

I beamed and threw my slider around the rope leading to the third pillar. The far end of the rope was lower now, since we'd moved it up on our end as we'd climbed the long, broken bridge at the side of the fourth pillar. It would be a fast ride.

I jumped into the air on my slider, glancing past my shoulder at Yipes, who clapped and hollered for me.

"I'll be back before dark!" I cried.

When I reached the other side, I began what turned out to be a maddeningly long effort to find Jonezy. I searched the third pillar only to find that he'd gone to the second, but when I arrived at the second, I found that he'd gone to the first to oversee a harvest of one sort or another. Ranger caught sight of me and wouldn't leave my side. We took the rowboat across the lake together, searched the veranda, and made our way to the pond. When I finally found Jonezy near the windmills, Ranger pranced around with a stick in his mouth hoping one of us would throw it.

"I think I've thrown that stick a hundred times already today," I guessed.

"If only I had his get-up-and-go," said Jonezy.

"I think you've got plenty of energy," I said. "You've been walking two paces ahead of me all day. Thank goodness I finally found you. We need to talk."

Jonezy threw the stick into the middle of the pond.

"It takes him longer to swim than to run. This way he won't bother us so often."

And so it was that I stood by the windmills on the second pillar and told Jonezy everything as he tossed a stick for Ranger over and over again. I told him all about the fourth pillar, Sir Alistair Wakefield, his flying machine, and what he theorized about Abaddon's intent.

"I don't know if this place is going to survive," I said, saddened by the thought of losing such a magnificent place. "At least not in the same way that everyone has come to know it."

"If that monster succeeds in knocking down the fourth pillar and it hits the third, it will be a catastrophe. We can't lose that pillar, Alexa."

"I'm afraid it could be much worse than that," I said, wanting to make sure Jonezy understood how dire our situation really was. "By tomorrow, Abaddon may have shredded through enough of the fourth pillar to topple it. And what if it takes out not only the third, but the second and the first pillars as well?"

"Do you think that could really happen?" asked Jonezy, concern rising in his voice.

"Sir Alistair thinks there's a very real chance, especially if the third pillar is hit. It's thicker, so it might not snap in two, but who knows?"

Jonezy took stock of the situation and tossed the stick for the wet dog before him, watching Ranger bolt into the pond.

"It will be safest — and easiest — to meet everyone at the lake," he said after a moment. "I can have everyone at the shoreline in an hour."

He paused and took in a deep breath. Letting it out, his chest sank and his head dropped.

"This is going to be hard," he said. "Are you sure you're ready?"

"No," I said, not entirely ready to stand before hundreds of people and tell them their way of life might be coming to an end. "But I've got no choice. When they find out who I am, hopefully they'll listen."

Jonezy began to walk toward the lake and Ranger followed, shaking his wet coat from head to tail.

"Oh, Jonezy — one thing more," I said. "We're going to do a test flight after dark so Abaddon can't watch what we're doing. It will only make him work faster if he thinks we have an escape plan. If he could be distracted — so we're sure he won't discover what we're up to — it would help. How's it going with Phylo?"

"He's gathering rocks by the hundreds and the best shooters he can find. I think we can provide a nice diversion for you tonight. It should be quite a show."

"That's just what I wanted to hear," I said.

One of the nice things about a society living in a small space is that you can gather everyone together quickly. The Five Stone Pillars was just such a place, where people of all ages could be scattered between just three places — the first, second, and third pillars. Within an hour's time, the whole world could be at your doorstep, waiting for you to open your mouth.

"Are you *sure* you're ready to do this?" whispered Jonezy. "I can do the talking if you'd rather. We don't have to tell them about . . ."

I touched Jonezy on his forearm, furry with gray hair, and I glanced up into the sky. Soon the sun would be on the horizon and I'd be expected back at the fourth pillar. "I'm ready," I said.

Jonezy turned to the crowd that stood along the

shore of the lake. There were, in my estimation, an equal share of children, adults, and those moving into later adulthood, all of whom would have known Roland and Thomas at the House on the Hill so many years before.

"Let's all gather in close, if we could," said Jonezy. Everyone stirred and the two toddlers in the group were picked up and held by two mothers I hadn't met. The three girls that had befriended me only the night before — had it been that recently? — stood near and waved to me. I waved back and smiled. Scanning the audience I saw Phylo as well, acting rather kingly among a group of boys his own age. He'd obviously brought them into his planned attack on the sea monster.

"As you all know, Alexa arrived here with a companion only a few days ago. You've welcomed them into our way of life and tried to make them feel at home, and for that I know she's thankful."

I nodded, feeling a genuine sense of gratitude.

"You also know that she brought things with her we have had a hard time understanding — a strange creature that doesn't seem to like us very much, some bad news about Roland Warvold and the *Warwick Beacon*, questions about the future of the Five Stone Pillars. I've met with her privately to find out what I could, and now she would like to address you all herself."

Jonezy stood aside, and I was at once terrified to speak and certain of what needed to be said. It wouldn't be easy, but I knew it would have to start with me opening my mouth.

I began, "I wish I had more time to meet all of you and explore every corner of the Five Stone Pillars, but my arrival comes at a perilous moment. Unfortunately, time is not something we can take for granted."

There was whispering then, and I felt some concern that they didn't believe me.

"I didn't intend to come here as a messenger with bad news, or to bring terrible things to pass. What happened to Roland and the *Warwick Beacon* was so unexpected — and what came along with us — even Roland didn't know a monster was tracking our every move."

"I've seen the monster!" cried Phylo. By now everyone had seen it, but Phylo was particularly excited.

"And Phylo has devised an ingenious way of fighting it," I added. Phylo beamed with pride.

"I've helped defeat this monster before — in a different form — but I don't see how it can be defeated again. I'm afraid no amount of fighting we do will push this beast back into the Lonely Sea forever. It comes to do something worse than destroy the Five Stone Pillars. It comes to rule this place."

"Rule, you say?" came a voice from a middle-aged man who wore a wide-rimmed hat tied with a string. "Is that really possible?"

"I know it seems as if Abaddon . . ." Did they even

know who Abaddon was? I couldn't be sure, and I didn't want to confuse them, but looking at many of their faces told me they were quite aware of who was embodied by the sea monster below.

"You've brought the evil of the whole world upon us," said a young woman.

"But Abaddon can't be in two places at once," said another. "Does this mean Castalia is free?"

Finally, some good news to report!

"Yes! I was there. Victor Grindall and his ogres are defeated. Abaddon was thrown from The Land of Elyon, never to return. The unforeseen part of this victory is that Abaddon took the form of a sea monster, the very one that's trying to tear down the fourth pillar."

There was a rumbling of talk — some good, some not so good — and many speculated about Castalia, The Land of Elyon, and their old lives.

"The sea monster is far below and can do you no harm all the way up here. But it's more powerful than you suppose. I think it may knock down the fourth pillar as early as tomorrow, and that pillar could fall in any direction."

Murmuring of concern worked its way through the crowd, and some shouted their disbelief at such an unlikely outcome.

"Sir Alistair Wakefield himself thinks the pillar won't last another day."

I blurted this out a little sooner and a little faster than I had originally planned, and it resulted in many questions being asked all at one time.

He's alive? Where did you see him? What did he say?

"Everyone calm down!" Jonezy yelled. "She can't answer all your questions at once."

The crowd quieted and I told them all about my encounter with Sir Alistair, that he was in fact alive, and that Matilda, Yipes, and Marco were on the fourth pillar helping him.

"We thought he was dead!" a chorus of voices echoed.

"I've been hearing that a lot," I offered. "He seems very . . . private. I guess he just wanted to be alone so that he could work. He's trying to help you — we all are."

A young, strong-looking man came forward. He was one of the fisherman who hauled giant nets from the sea. His arms and hands were heavy with muscle.

"Even if the fourth pillar could be knocked down — and that seems wholly impossible to me — it's by far the thinnest of them all. Abaddon couldn't possibly knock down any of the pillars we live on."

"What if the fourth pillar falls into the third?" I asked. "Then what?"

There was a gasp from the crowd at the thought of damage done to the skimming pillar. The fisherman laughed through his nose at first, but then he appeared to be calculating what might happen in the event that the fourth actually did impact the third.

"That's exactly where the fourth is going to fall if it comes down," I continued. "That's the side Abaddon is ripping stone out of. What if the impact of the fourth pillar falling were to break the third pillar of stone? It might just tip into the second, and then the first. I know this creature, and if my guess is right, that's precisely what it aims to do. It tore the *Warwick Beacon* to pieces in a matter of minutes. I believe it has the power to tear down pillars of stone."

"That's impossible!" cried the fisherman. But even as he said it, his face showed some doubt, and everyone around him seemed convinced it could happen.

"Even if this doesn't come to pass, it won't matter. If Abaddon wants to rule this place and he can get to the top of one of these pillars, then I'm afraid the Five Stone Pillars are doomed. He'll find those among us he can manipulate and control. He'll set us against one another and bring ruin until he takes everything and turns the whole place as evil as he is. That's his goal."

"We can't let him do it!" a chorus of angry voices sounded the same idea back and forth between the group.

"Then fight as hard as you can to save this place. Use the method Phylo has come up with and deter that monster for as long as you can. But be realistic. Barring a miracle, he can't be stopped, and even if the fourth pillar falls dead into the sea, he'll just begin again on the next pillar until he gets what he wants. It could take him years to chew through the third pillar, but that doesn't mean he won't keep going until he knocks it down. Or the fourth pillar may crash into the third, only to stay leaning there, an easier path for the monster to come ashore."

More chattering filled the air at the thought. Oddly — and it had only just occurred to me — the third pillar was in many ways a tailor-made home for a beast such as the monster that lurked below. It was a pillar covered in an intricate, weblike system of vines. The top was concave, thus hidden from view should anyone pass by. Abaddon was a many-armed creature in the water, so it would make sense for him to be a many-armed spider on land. Maybe he had known about the third pillar all along and wanted it for his home.

"How many children live on the Five Stone Pillars?" I asked. "Those under twelve or thirteen years old."

Jonezy answered. "There are, I think, about thirty. The youngest is two, and a handful are five or six. We have a good number of eight- to ten-year-olds and a few on up to twelve."

"We should move the youngest of them if we can," I said.

"How do you mean to move them?" asked one of the mothers. I could tell she was a mother because she held one of the few very young children. Everyone who had arrived on the stone pillars by way of the *Warwick Beacon* had come to it as an orphan, rescued from a past Castalia ruled by evil. Only a very few children had actually been born here.

I was about to say something I wasn't sure would go over very well, but I had to say it at some point, and the time had come, whether I wanted to do it or not.

"I think I have a way," I began. "To bring you all back home."

More gasps — some angry, some excited — and a chorus of protests and questions followed.

You mean we can go back to The Land of Elyon? How will we get there? You're not taking the children! We're not going anywhere!

"Give the girl a chance!" said Jonezy. "Let her explain before you make up your minds."

And so I continued as best and as honestly as I could.

"Sir Alistair has been working on something for a very long time, and he thinks it can get us home. We're going to test it tonight, and I'll know more in the morning. That's all I can say right now. But it could hold the children if you wanted to have them taken to safety. They could return to a renewed Castalia."

"We're not putting these children on a boat with that thing down there!" someone cried.

"It's not a boat. It's . . . something else."

"What kind of something? Tell us what you mean to do with the children!"

I couldn't tell them that we were flying home, like a bird. They'd never believe me, and it sounded too dangerous. I'd have to show them when and if the time came.

"Trust me — please — I simply can't tell you. I don't even know if it will work. But I'll know tomorrow. I promise to tell you then."

An older woman of about the same age as Jonezy stepped forward out of the crowd.

"Why did Roland bring you with him into the Lonely Sea?" she asked. And then a more direct question, "Who are you?"

The words rang in my ears. There would never be a better time to tell them who I was.

"Roland had a brother — there were just the two of them — you all must know that."

"Of course we know it," said the fisherman with the giant arms who had so vigorously opposed me only a moment ago. "Some among us knew them both at the House on the Hill. We've heard the legends. If it wasn't for them, we'd have rotted on that hill of garbage and a lot of us would have fallen by the hand of Victor Grindall. We keep all those stories alive here. We don't forget."

"I'm glad to hear that," I said. "And I'm so very sorry that the time of the Warvolds has passed. Thomas and Roland are gone, but I remain."

The crowd fell deathly silent, as if they had just been told that Roland was alive and about to walk out of the trees and stand before them as their leader once more.

"What are you saying?" asked the fisherman, but he seemed to have figured it out on his own and his voice trembled.

"She's saying," said Jonezy, "that she is Thomas Warvold's daughter."

"Is this true?" asked one of the three girls who had befriended me. She was very excited.

I nodded. "I am called Alexa Daley because I was hidden away for a time, but my father was Thomas Warvold."

There was something eminently powerful about these words. As I said them I felt different, as if they held weight I hadn't previously understood. It wasn't that the crowd bowed down and lined up to kiss my hand, but there was a genuine change in the tone of everything. There were tiny, almost hidden smiles. The Warvold name and all it had meant had power I didn't realize — the power of myth and legend. All at once I knew they would listen and that I'd given them something to hold on to. I had given them hope. I had gotten them thinking about how it might, in the end and under the right circumstances, be okay to leave their home.

I insisted that I be left on my own to find my way back to the fourth pillar. I needed time to think things through, and the people of the Five Stone Pillars would benefit from my absence as they thought through decisions of their own. I made the long walk back to the fourth pillar and left Jonezy, Phylo, Ranger, and the rest to their business. When I was alone, I spoke the name of Elyon over and over again, hoping against hope that good would yet prevail.

I had been told that my days of hearing Elyon's voice were behind me until I reached the very end at the gates of the Tenth City. But it still surprised me that I felt alone at the outset of a great battle. Would Elyon come to my aid, or was I truly on my own this time?

CHAPTER 18
STARGAZER

I made quick work of the bridge from the second to the third pillar. Finding no one at the third pillar on my arrival was eerie and troublesome. I looked down at the empty, crisscrossing vines and could think only of an enormous, metal-headed spider turning everything black. I could imagine the beauty of the third pillar with its cottages against a sea of green turning dead and lifeless. The third pillar was too quiet — no hollering as skimmers flew past, no buzz of activity from the village below — and I had a premonition of its demise that frightened me.

I placed my slider over the nearest vine and jumped clean and free into the air. It was different with no one around, scarier for some reason, and I couldn't shake the idea that Abaddon was lurking in the vines, already transformed into a spider of massive proportion.

For once, I was happy for my flight to end at the other side. I advanced quickly on the hill and found the rope leading to the fourth pillar. There was no one waiting for me at the other side, and looking down into the water I saw that Abaddon was my only company.

What are you up to, Alexa Daley?

I was feeling bold and angry, and it showed in my response.

"You'll never rule this place. But if you leave now, we'll let you alone in the Lonely Sea."

There was a tremendous howling laughter from below.

I've grown weary of the water. It's cold. Very soon you and I will change places!

And then Abaddon climbed twenty feet or more up the side of the pillar, his arms extending out longer than I'd seen them extend before. Flames licked in every direction. There was the sound of metal on stone as Abaddon smashed his many arms into the pillar and tore boulder-sized chunks free. He held on to a rock as big as the cart I used to ride between Lathbury and Bridewell, and his body began to shake. Everything about Abaddon turned red and fiery. The stone itself began to glow red with the force of Abaddon's anger until all at once it exploded into a thousand pieces and the sound of despicable laughter filled the air.

You should be careful who you trust. You might be surprised how many people I can turn against you!

"You're a liar!" I screamed, angrier and more confused than ever. I hastily took my slider in hand, flipped it over the rope leading to the fourth pillar, and dove into the air. It was a long way across, almost a minute to the other side, and looking down I watched as Abaddon attacked the pillar more ferociously than I'd ever seen him do so. His arms moved stunningly fast, hurling rocks up into the air toward me and tearing stone away like an ax against the base of a dying tree. As I reached the halfway point, the fourth pillar began to sway and rumble as if it might topple over. It had the effect of making the rope swing violently from side to side. Abaddon laughed and laughed, filling my head with the terrible sound of death coming to find me and hurl me into the Lonely Sea.

Abaddon stopped suddenly and the pillar settled down, but the rope remained turbulent as I approached the stone wall of the fourth pillar. I was coming in extremely fast and my legs were swinging from side to side. I couldn't get them out in front of me fast enough, and I'd waited too long to begin slowing down by twisting my slider.

And now I wait. This pillar is about to fall, but it will fall at my choosing, when I make it so.

Those were the last words of Abaddon I heard as he slipped back into the Lonely Sea, sizzling on the water as he disappeared from view. I gripped my slider as tightly as I could and hit the pillar shoulder first, bouncing back into the air. I felt as though I'd been dropped flat on my back onto a cobblestone road from a great height. The wind was knocked out of me and I couldn't breathe. Stars and blackness filled my vision as I told myself one thing over and over again: *Hold on! Hold on! Hold on, Alexa!*

But I couldn't hold on. I couldn't even breathe. The slider began to slip slowly from my fingers even as my feet tangled in the rope bridge before me. When I finally let go, I fell backward, out toward the Lonely Sea. The shock of this feeling — of knowing I was about to fly free one last time — pushed me back to breathing. I managed to get my hands facing the pillar and protected my head, for my feet were tangled in the rope ladder and they held. I was injured and upside down, but I was alive and holding steady on the side of the fourth stone pillar.

It took some careful thinking to get myself turned back around and to work my way up the ladder. My whole body shook with fear at each painful step, but I couldn't help thinking that climbing now felt very much like the first time I'd climbed up the ladder to the library in Bridewell from out of the hidden tunnels. Back then I had only just returned from meeting Yipes for the first time, from hearing the voice of Darius the wolf, from an adventure that seemed, at times, more play than real. How was it that I'd found my way across the Lonely Sea to a place so unreal, in a battle so far beyond my abilities?

"Are you all right?" came a familiar voice from above.

"Yipes!" I cried, looking up and seeing the silhouette of my best friend's hat against the blue sky.

"Take it slow," he said as I raced up the ladder. "Who knows what this pillar might do next?"

197

He took my hand at the top and pulled me up. Having him hold my hand made me realize that I'd lost my slider coming across.

"I don't have a slider," I said. "I dropped mine."

"Maybe you won't need it to get back across," said Yipes. He had a sly look on his face, like he knew something he couldn't wait for me to see. "Come on. The sun will be setting soon. And with night comes the first flight."

I groaned as we started up the side of the fourth pillar.

"Can I take off my sandals?" I asked.

Yipes nodded and I carefully took them off, holding them both in one hand.

"Does this feel familiar to you?" I asked.

"What do you mean?"

I squished my toes into green moss and we climbed.

"Don't you remember when we first met? You led me to the secret pool to find one of the last Jocastas. I took my sandals off then, and I walked in the water on green moss. My body hurt then as it does now, in a new way that I didn't think I could hurt."

"I guess you're right," said Yipes. "Everything about this place is so different and yet so much like the places we've been before."

My strength was returning as we went on. It occurred to me then that it was in times of struggle that I found the best parts of myself — courage, loyalty, an unexpected peace — and I always discovered what I needed to break through and go on.

"The Five Stone Pillars have the fingerprints of Elyon all over them," I said. "He made this place — I'm sure of it. He's not going to let Abaddon have it in the end."

Yipes nodded his agreement as we reached the edge of the hole leading to Sir Alistair's chamber. Nimbus was sitting on the other side and appeared to be waiting for us.

"It's cloudy on the horizon this evening," she purred. "I like the clouds."

"How long before dark?" asked Yipes. Cats had a way of knowing such things rather precisely.

"Less than an hour," meowed Nimbus. "Cutting it close, aren't we?"

I didn't feel at all like arguing with a cat, so I sat down and slid into the hole, leaving Nimbus to wonder what I was thinking.

In my absence, the flying machine had been successfully prepared for its first flight out of Sir Alistair's chamber. It was plump full of air, bobbing gently overhead, and it seemed to me as if the balloon wanted to be let off its leash to roam free on the air above.

"You're back!" said Matilda. She came near and we couldn't help hugging each other.

"Yipes has been so much help," she told me. "He's been climbing up and down the ropes of the balloon making sure she's ready."

"What about me?" said Marco, yelling from one of the platforms above.

Matilda rolled her eyes and whispered to me, "He's actually been doing quite a lot."

I discovered that it had been Marco — not Yipes — who'd carried most of the moss from the outside into the chamber. And Sir Alistair had taught him how to shave the underside free, bake it in the oven in a special container, and sift it into green dust.

"How far will that get us?" I asked as I came over to the large box beneath the balloon and saw three full jars of green.

"I'm not certain," said Sir Alistair. "Until we fly her, we won't know how much it will take to keep her afloat."

All this talk of *her* and *she* made me feel like it was high time we gave *her* a name.

"Roland was very fond of the *Warwick Beacon*," I said. "I think the name made it more real."

"I wholeheartedly agree," said Yipes, glancing up at the bobbing balloon. "What shall we call her?"

Yipes, Matilda, and I all looked at the strange wings along the sides of the box, the rudders at the back, the many vines leading up into the chamber that held the round balloon. But Sir Alistair was looking beyond to the gathering night. It was he who said the name, as if he had chosen it long ago on a night much like this one.

"*Stargazer*," he whispered, and we all repeated the name. It was perfect.

Sir Alistair looked longingly at *Stargazer*, then pronounced the day about to turn to night.

"I've decided on the team that will navigate the first flight," he said. "We need a crew of three, and here is how it shall go."

Sir Alistair Wakefield saved authoritative tones of voice for when he really meant them, and never had I heard him quite so certain about what he was about to say. When he made an invention — it appeared — he would have it used the way he chose or not used at all. I was determined not to argue, even if by some miserable chance of fate Marco's name would be spoken in the chamber.

"Alexa, you will be at *Stargazer*'s helm, guiding the movement. It is for you she was made, just as the *Warwick Beacon* was made for your uncle Roland. You and you alone must guide this ship of the air. I have a hunch it will require a soft touch and a flying instinct, both of which I believe you possess. This vessel is yours, Alexa, with my blessing. I'm pleased that circumstances have made it possible for you to have the crew you will need to make the most of it."

I beamed at the thought of sailing *Stargazer* through the air. Already I thought of her less as a machine and more as an extension of myself.

"And you," Sir Alistair said, turning his piercing gaze on Yipes. "You are a gift from Elyon if ever there was one. It is you that must be first mate on this first and — I hope — many future voyages. Flying *Stargazer* will, no doubt, include many complications. Vines will fray and come loose, birds will pierce the balloon, the anchor will need to be dropped in unexpected places, and so much more. There will be times when she will seem to have a mind of her own and she will need to be tamed. You alone have the instincts and the uncommon agility to help guide this vessel."

Yipes took off his hat — which he rarely did — and bowed before Sir Alistair. He reached out for Sir Alistair's hand and Sir Alistair didn't know quite what to do.

"You're welcome," he said, hoping this would be enough. But Yipes was undeterred. He grasped Sir Alistair's hand and shook it vigorously as he so liked to do.

"I won't fail you."

"I'm certain you won't," said Sir Alistair, but Yipes kept shaking and shaking.

"Do you suppose I could have my hand back?"

"Certainly!" said Yipes, who let go and bounded up onto the rail of the box all by himself, already at the business of checking the ropes.

"Marco," said Sir Alistair. My heart sank at the thought of having Marco and not Matilda on the flight, and I nearly objected at the very sound of his name. Sir Alistair stopped short, looked outside, and realized the sun was about to set on the horizon. "Marco," he went on, repeating the name I didn't want to hear, "do you think you could handle the wings and the rudders?"

"What?!" I yelled, finally overcome by disappointment. "But what about Matilda? Why can't she guide the wings?"

Sir Alistair didn't have to answer. He could have looked at me with those piercing eyes and put me in my place. He'd built *Stargazer* and it was his to do with as he pleased. He knew better — and yet he must have known I'd protest. Maybe he even knew I had to learn to trust the people and the things I didn't want to in order to captain my own ship.

"Alexa," he began, and in a soft, wispy voice he explained that manning the wings and the rudders required someone with stamina and great strength. There was a time and a place for the large and small among us — or so he said — and this particular task needed someone who could turn the wheels and move the handles with precision and speed.

"But I don't trust him. He tried to kill me once already!"

"Did not!" yelled Marco.

Sir Alistair glanced back and forth between me and Marco. I couldn't be sure if he believed me or not.

"You'll have to work it out. Marco it is, and that's final."

Sir Alistair knelt down and picked up Midnight, who was leaning against his leg purring.

"And, you — are you ready for your first flight?"

"I've been waiting almost as long as you have," meowed Midnight. "I'm more than ready."

I couldn't believe my ears. Over half my crew was made up of people or animals I didn't trust.

"You've got to be kidding," I protested. "Why do we need a cat on board?"

"Because animals can sense danger in ways we humans cannot. They'll tell you if the weather is about to change."

"What do you mean *they?*" I asked, afraid of what he was going to say next.

"Nimbus is going, too. She's especially good at sniffing out bad weather on the way."

"But what about Matilda? I want her to come along." I thought I'd earned at least the right to bring along someone else I actually liked.

"I need Matilda here, to help me release the balloon and guide you back in. Her part is as important as any other."

I wished she could come along, but Matilda smiled faintly and said everything would be okay, that she'd be waiting to bring me back in safely. I was all out of arguments and the sun had finally set. Night had come to the Five Stone Pillars, and with it, the first flight. Marco and Yipes lit lamps all around the entrance and throughout the chamber, giving the room a ghostly quality as I looked out at a sky filling with stars.

We spent the next few minutes going over the

controls, on which Marco had evidently spent a lot of time practicing in my absence. It was maddening to feel that he knew *Stargazer* better than I did. Sir Alistair guided us all to our posts. There was a seat that swiveled where I was to sit, and it would be my job to add green powder to the tube when I felt it was needed. Marco had a strange seat all his own, one that included a place for his feet to turn fans and handles for his hands to adjust the wings at the sides of the box and the rudders at the back.

Yipes had no seat of his own. He was expected to be moving about frantically, observing the wings and climbing up and down ropes, checking everything as we went. He was also in charge of the anchor, which was held on a long rope, and he could climb up and down additional ropes that hung from the top of the balloon and along the sides of the box. Nimbus and Midnight had posts at corners of the box, where they sat quietly, watching all that took place.

"Is everyone ready?" asked Sir Alistair. "You must be quiet as mice out there, and don't stay out too long. We only want to test the balloon and bring it back quickly. If it works as I have supposed, the real flight will take place at dawn."

"I have a strong feeling the fourth pillar won't last past tomorrow," I said, thinking of what Abaddon had said as I tried to cross over. "We should be prepared by first light just in case."

"Your goal is to maneuver *Stargazer*, to get used to the way it flies, and to see how much powder it takes to keep it airborne without sinking closer to the sea."

Sir Alistair took a handful of dried moss and rubbed it between his hands until it was hardly more than dust. He walked to the low rail that stood before the opening to the outside. There was one place along the very edge of the opening where a platform ran out over the open water. There were rails along its side, but it didn't look at all sturdy. I hadn't seen anyone use it, but now Sir Alistair Wakefield walked right out into the open air. My heart caught in my throat because it had the strange appearance of someone floating, held up by nothing at all. Sir Alistair tossed the mossy dust into the air and watched. The wind carried it a little to the right.

"The wind is low, but it will try to push you south. Don't let it push you too far, or it will be difficult to make your way back again. Marco, you may need to pedal hard against the current of air in order to hold *Stargazer* steady."

"That won't be a problem," he said. He was so very sure of himself — I almost wished we would drift far to the south just so I could see him fail.

Sir Alistair took one last look at his marvelous invention and addressed Yipes.

"Is everything at the ready?"

"A moment for a final inspection, if you please,"

Yipes answered. He stared at Marco and the cats, assessing their positions. Walking along the rim of the box, he twanged ropes and knocked on wood. When finally he'd made it all the way around, he looked me up and down with a wary eye.

"I believe she's ready, sir!"

I wasn't sure if he was talking about me or *Stargazer*.

"At your command then, Alexa," said Sir Alistair. He had a faraway look in his eye, as if he'd waited for this moment a long time and had dreamed about what might happen.

It was up to me now. I sat in the seat that was my calling, looked out into the open air, and gave the command.

"Let her fly."

CHAPTER 19

FIRST FLIGHT

Stargazer was already fat with hot air, tugging on the ropes like she was listening in on our conversation. I felt she was more than a flying contraption, that *Stargazer* had a mind of her own and a spirit that wanted to be let free on the wind. She had stayed put for far too long, like a bear tied to a chain in that story Roland told me on the Lonely Sea.

Matilda and Sir Alistair unhitched ropes from the floor on two opposite corners, leaving three more ropes holding *Stargazer* inside the chamber. There were ropes on the two other corners still, plus one longer rope attached to a more elaborate pulley system so that we could be let out, as on a long leash.

"Take that one in your hands," Sir Alistair told Matilda, pointing her toward one of the two opposite tie-downs. "But don't hold too tight. If she takes off, the rope will burn through your hands."

Matilda nodded and unlaced the knot that held the rope around a small loop in the rock floor of the chamber. Sir Alistair did the same, and when he was sure there was just the one rope attached to the pulley, he nodded in my direction.

"Start the fans," I said, and Marco began pedaling the wheel inside the box, holding his hands steady on the two bars that controlled the rudders.

Stargazer lurched forward and the box rocked back and forth. She really wanted to fly!

"Slow down — not so fast," I said. For the first time since I'd met him, Marco not only complied with my command but seemed genuinely pleased that someone else was in charge of what could become a very dangerous situation. He slowed the fans, watching me for the sign that he'd settled into the right cadence.

"A little to the left," I said. Marco gently pushed the bar that controlled the left rudder and slowed his pedaling to a crawl. *Stargazer* settled, straight and true, and Marco laughed nervously at his own effort.

"Better let us go," I said to Sir Alistair. "She's ready to rise."

Sir Alistair and Matilda released the ropes at once, leaving just the one in the middle. The box rose awkwardly off the ground and the cats clawed into wood in order to hold on. Yipes swung around a corner rope leading up to the balloon and settled in on the rail. We were off the ground, heading for the opening over the Lonely Sea, and I felt a perfect balance of calm and exhilaration I'd only dreamed of in my long past of adventuring. I knew then that I would do whatever I must to spend the rest of my life flying *Stargazer*.

"Faster!" I cried. "Bring us out!"

Marco sped up the fans, pedaling and adjusting the rudders so that we were moving straight for the giant opening into the night.

"That's perfect, Marco," I said, feeling the rope on the pulley letting us out a little bit at a time. It was a good feeling knowing the rope held us firm and that it would pull us back inside after we'd had a chance to play with the controls and learn how *Stargazer* would respond to my commands.

"Keep letting us out slowly," I yelled down to Sir Alistair. We were already ten feet off the ground and Sir Alistair worked with the tension on the pulley, keeping us steadily moving out. It was apparent that we wouldn't need any powder for a while, and that *Stargazer* would travel wonderfully without feeding her too much. This was good news.

We approached the opening in perfect position, with plenty of room on all sides to slip out over the Lonely Sea. As soon as we were free, I felt the soft wind on the balloon as we drifted to the right. It felt as if *Stargazer* knew she had emerged from a long slumber, for she pulled harder on the rope that held us. I looked back into the chamber with its glowing lamps, and Sir Alistair nodded that the rope and pulley were holding just fine.

I heard a splashing below and leaned out over the box.

"Look there!" said Yipes. Marco was seated and couldn't leave his post, but Yipes and I both saw the flurry of green rocks flying toward the base of the fourth stone pillar. Phylo and his team were firing countless stones of glowing green at Abaddon. It was a marvelous sight from our vantage point, like an endless shower of falling stars with long shimmering tails.

"They're really making a go of it," said Yipes.

But I knew Abaddon was finished coming above the water until he chose. He was waiting below, waiting for one final blow at a time of his choosing, and I didn't expect to see him. It was this feeling I had — that I didn't expect him — that made his voice in my head all the more surprising.

You have been a good servant. Now cut the rope.

"What's he saying?" I said. Marco, Yipes, even the cats — they all looked at me in the dim starlight as if I'd gone mad.

"What did *who* say?" asked Marco.

The command came again.

That's it! Cut the rope! Leave them to drift into the Lonely Sea!

What was Abaddon saying? I ran all the scenarios through my head and tried to imagine what it could mean. Cut the rope? There was only one rope, held by the pulley and controlled by Sir Alistair. There was only one other person who —

"NO!" I cried. "Don't do it, Matilda!"

Looking back into the chamber, I saw that Matilda had pulled out a knife and was slicing hard and fast against the rope that held us. Sir Alistair was lying on the ground. What had she done to him?

"Matilda, no! Don't listen to him!"

She looked up and I saw from a distance that she was entranced, not under her own control. I thought back to the night skim and my broken slider. Could it have been Matilda? And the first landing at the fourth pillar — the one that had gone badly — could she have been trying to do away with me? I recalled that she had shaken her head, as if trying to shake a ghost out of her mind. What had he said to her? *The way of yesterday is not for you. She has brought you to a place you should not have come. But not to worry. She won't be with you much longer!*

She had been hearing Abaddon's voice all along.

"You don't have to do what he says," I shouted. "You can fight him!"

But Matilda couldn't hear my plea. She went back to cutting the rope.

"Grump! Stop her!" Yipes screamed. Grump began moving toward Matilda in the glimmering light of the chamber, but it was too late.

Good-bye, Alexa Daley. I almost wish you could be here come morning, so you could see what I'm going to do to this place. But you'll be long gone by then.

The rope snapped in two and whipped through the air. *Stargazer* felt the release, and we were at once rising faster, moving out to sea with alarming speed.

"What now?" meowed Midnight in that maddeningly

212

calm way that cats have about them, as if they really do have nine lives and could stand to waste one.

And it wasn't just Midnight looking to me for guidance. Everyone on the vessel — Yipes, Nimbus, Midnight, Marco — stared at me. I was *Stargazer's* captain, a post that was made especially for times like this. And yet I had no idea what I should do. My friend had come under the power of the enemy, Sir Alistair's fate was uncertain, and we were drifting out to sea on a contraption I had no experience controlling.

Sometimes unforeseen disaster has a way of clearing my mind, and seeing what we were heading straight for provided just the jump start I needed.

"The fifth pillar!" I yelled. Everyone turned to look, and they realized at once that we were heading straight for the jagged side of the tallest pillar of them all. If we didn't change course quickly, the balloon would hit sharp stone and tear wide open. That would be the end of *Stargazer* and the whole lot of us.

"Hard to the right, Marco! And pedal with all your might!"

Marco sprung into action, pulling down hard on the right rudder and pedaling so fast his feet became a blur of motion. We turned and the wings caught a mighty breeze, fluttering as if they might tear into pieces.

"Let's push a little more hot air into that balloon," I said to Yipes. He had been shown how to adjust the flow of hot air through the tube at the center of the box. Yipes

213

was swiftly at the controls, turning what looked like a smaller version of the wheel that had been at the helm of the *Warwick Beacon*. The sound of steam releasing filled the box and hot air shot up into the balloon.

"Faster, Marco!" I cried. We were still on a collision course with the fifth pillar, a hundred feet from crashing into it. The first thing to go would be the wing, crumpled against a wall of rock. Yipes grabbed hold of a long pole with a round head of wood on either end and leaped for one of the ropes leading up to the balloon.

"What's that for?" I questioned, but Yipes was climbing so fast I couldn't be sure he'd heard me.

"It's for pushing against obstacles," meowed Nimbus. "Like a stone pillar."

"So the balloon won't touch," I said.

"We're going too fast for it to be of any use," said Marco. "He's going to get hurt up there!"

"Just keep pedaling and pull a little more to the right."

I was trying to get *Stargazer* on a diagonal course away from the fifth pillar, so that we were moving out of its way while we were pushing against the wind at the same time. It was like paddling a boat upstream, but if we could hold steady long enough, we might drift to the side of the pillar and just miss it.

"I'm getting tired," wheezed Marco. "Not sure I can keep this pace much longer."

"We're almost past. A little more!" I cried.

In the dim light of stars and flying green rocks, the fifth tower was a black mass that threatened to make *Stargazer's* first flight its last. I couldn't see Yipes from where I sat — he'd gone up the side of the balloon and I had no way of knowing how far.

"That's it, Marco — you're doing it!" I yelled. "Pull hard to the right now and I think we can shoot past."

Marco's chest was heaving but he kept at it, yanking down on the control stick. We stopped paddling upstream with the fans and drove straight across the face of the fifth stone pillar. The balloon and the wings extended beyond the box by a good twenty feet on both sides, and it appeared that we weren't going to make it. The balloon was going to touch first — only barely — but enough that it would be sliced through by the sharp rocks of the rising cliffs.

"Pull in the wings! Now!" I commanded.

Marco let go of the rudder controls and placed his hands below the sides of the seat, pulling up on wooden handles with all his might. The wings crept in tighter to the box, leaving only the balloon in harm's way.

I waited, sure that I'd failed everyone with my timing, but the sound of ripping didn't come. In fact, we drifted right around the edge and kept on going, along the far side of the fifth stone pillar. For the moment, we were out of danger.

Out of sheer excitement I grabbed Marco by the shoulders and shook him, laughing and congratulating him on his success.

Yipes came sliding down one of the ropes with the pole tucked under one arm.

"That was close," he said. "But this thing really works. Sir Alistair thought of everything. The pole, you see — it pushes the balloon in on itself and away from danger at the same time. Simple but brilliant."

"Well done, Yipes," said Marco, though he was catching his breath and it was hard to understand what he was saying.

"And you as well!" said Yipes. He walked right up to Marco and stuck his tiny hand out. "I've misjudged you. Forgive me for accusing you without any true evidence."

"Apology accepted," said Marco. He looked at me then, expecting the same, and I had to admit he'd redeemed himself. We'd judged him pretty harshly, and all along something very different had been going on. Abaddon had managed to turn us against Marco — and Matilda against us. It was Abaddon I should have been trying to figure out all along.

"I'm sorry for being rash — for not giving you a chance," I said. "Now let's figure out a way to turn *Stargazer* around and land her. We need to go back for Sir Alistair and Grump and Matilda."

"Are you sure you want to go back for her?" asked Marco.

216

"It's not Matilda who's doing these terrible things. It's that monster down there. I can fix this."

Yipes came near me with eyes that were both sad and hopeful.

"I think I may want to . . ." Yipes stopped short, not sure if he should go on. He obviously liked Matilda very much. "We need to get her back."

I nodded. "Do we all feel we can handle *Stargazer*?" I asked.

Everyone — even the cats — replied without hesitation that they could indeed manage the flight of a gigantic flying machine.

"Let's take *Stargazer* around the back side of the fifth stone pillar. The wind is dying down and we can come around the other side."

We charted a course back to the fourth pillar and hoped that we could land *Stargazer* without incident, retrieve Matilda from the clutches of Abaddon, and make our way back into the sky before dawn.

But we were running out of time. . . .

CHAPTER 20

MONSTER SCALE

It took longer than I would have hoped to maneuver around the fifth pillar and carefully manage the movements of *Stargazer*. She really did buck and pitch like a wild stallion that needed taming, like she knew where she wanted to go and wouldn't be told otherwise. But Marco and Yipes were becoming a skilled team. They knew how to bring *Stargazer* into line — to harness her power and will — and to move us in the direction we had to go.

Beneath the wooden rail, there was a line of small lamps, and I was studying the maps and the expected winds that would come as the days turned to weeks and the long summer dragged on. I was already thinking about how I would manage a journey across the Lonely Sea, *Stargazer* filled with children on their way home. What if I crashed or ran out of powder fuel? What then? The thought of being responsible for so many made me wonder if I could handle a long voyage. I wasn't even sure I could land *Stargazer*, let alone run her for weeks on end across open water.

"What time do you suppose it is?" Marco asked. He'd been steadily pedaling the fans for more than an hour on our loop around the fifth pillar. We'd left the chamber late, at around half past ten, because days lasted a long time in midsummer on the Lonely Sea. The sun would begin rising in the east shortly after four in the morning.

"It could be midnight, but I don't think it's quite that late yet," I said.

"If it's nearing midnight, we only have four hours to get everyone off the fourth pillar," said Yipes.

We were approaching the gigantic opening to the chamber and its gathering of brightly burning lights. There had been no sound from Abaddon for a while. Maybe he was dreaming of our demise, resting before a final assault on the Five Stone Pillars at the rising of the sun.

"We'll need to be hasty about things after we land," I said. I handed out a collection of responsibilities for everyone, including the cats (they were to get Grump into the box beneath the balloon).

"Slow her down, Marco," I instructed. Marco stopped pedaling — but only for a second — and then he was pedaling slowly in reverse, which made Stargazer sway heavily over our heads.

"A tiny bit of air, if you please," I said to Yipes. This was an important moment. The opening to the chamber was huge, but so was Stargazer. We were coming in straight and slow thanks to Marco's excellent command of the rudders, wings, and pedals, but we were a small bit lower than we needed to be. We would need to rise slightly in order to land.

"Bring in the wings."

Marco moved his hands skillfully at my command while Yipes tweaked one of the wooden handles at the tube gently open and shut again. *Stargazer* floated up ever so slightly. The wings tucked in. Then Yipes took hold of one of the tie-down ropes and jumped out of the box, into the open air. I wanted to yell for him, but knew I must be quiet as we entered. The last thing we wanted to do was wake the sleeping giant below and we weren't sure what sort of situation we were about to encounter with Matilda.

Yipes swung below the rim of the chamber, then up again. He had to lift his legs to avoid crashing into the pillar, but he was safely inside, pulling the rope toward the pulley that had once held it.

Looking all through the chamber, I saw that Sir Alistair was no longer lying on the ground. Neither he nor Matilda were anywhere to be seen, though Grump appeared to be sleeping near the pulley.

Yipes tied the rope back in place and began cranking the handle, bringing us in gently.

"Be careful down there," I said, releasing the cats into the chamber. Marco slid down a rope and began to tie us down as the cats slinked around looking for signs of Sir Alistair and Matilda.

"Where have they gone?" asked Midnight.

"I don't know," answered Nimbus. The two of them

220

went directly to Grump and asked him as I jumped out of *Stargazer* and looked around carefully.

"Well done, Yipes," said Marco. He sat down, exhausted from his effort at the pedals and the rudders.

"And you as well," said Yipes. My crew was getting along nicely, but there was no time for pleasantries.

"We have a lot to figure out," I said. "But first, we have to find them."

Marco was up again without hesitation. He and Yipes were to load food, water, powdered fuel, and saltwater into the box. After that, they would need to check over the rudders, gears, wings, and lines. We'd managed to bring *Stargazer* under our control, but there was a much longer journey in our future. We had to find Matilda and Sir Alistair and move things along, for dawn was but a few hours away.

"Over there," purred Midnight in her quietest voice. She was wrapped around my leg, looking off toward the vast model of the Wakefield House. "Grump told us where to look."

At the foot of the Wakefield House amid a glimmering of candlelight sat Sir Alistair Wakefield and Matilda. Sir Alistair was tied to a chair, his head slumped forward. Matilda sat next to him and watched our approach with eyes more asleep than awake.

"Don't get too close," said Nimbus. "She's of two minds."

Nimbus had a different sense of danger than I did, and I was aware that I had come to trust both her and Midnight without realizing it. When we came within a few paces of the table where she sat, Matilda spoke.

"He's not going to let us go."

I stopped short at the sound of her voice. She was so tired and sad.

"You don't know that," I said.

Matilda had a knife in her hand, watching it unthinkingly. Sir Alistair remained silent and unmoving.

"Something happened that I couldn't tell you before," said Matilda. "On the morning of your arrival."

She shivered softly. She was small, but I knew how incredibly strong and skilled she was. If she wanted to end Sir Alistair's life she could do it before we could do anything about it.

"Keep talking," I whispered. "Stay with us while Abaddon sleeps."

The sound of my voice seemed to calm her, and the idea of whispers made her, for whatever reason, take on a childlike tone of her own soft whispering.

"I saw you — there against the water, standing at the top of the highest mast."

Yipes and I glanced at each other and I secretly mouthed the words, *She's talking about you.*

"And I saw what you didn't see. From behind . . . a dreadful, rising arm of metal and fire. There no avoiding it."

Matilda looked up at Yipes then — the first time she'd taken her eyes off the knife.

"I caught the water at the bottom and skimmed slower. And on the upswing we touched, you and I. Do you remember?"

"I do," said Yipes. "And you picked me up. I was surprised by your strength."

"You don't weigh very much," whispered Matilda. It was a good sign that she was making light of her heroics. It must have meant that Abaddon really was sleeping below, or at least not paying close attention to her circumstance. Maybe he'd already tossed her aside, thinking that she was doomed at the coming of dawn anyway and was of no more use to him.

"Then what happened?" asked Yipes. He was ever so slowly moving toward her.

"He touched me," Matilda gasped. "He *wanted* to let us go for his own purpose. He could have batted us out of the air. But he only touched me. And then we were dragged up the side of the pillar out of his reach."

"Show me where he touched you," said Yipes. He walked within range of her to attack him with the knife. Then he held out his hand.

Matilda wavered, a momentary wild look in her eyes, and then she began to cry softly.

"I can't . . ." she began whispering. "I can't show you."

Tears streamed down Matilda's face as she looked upon someone who she clearly loved. She had found in Yipes a companion — they'd both known it from the moment they'd set eyes on each other — and yet she could not overcome the dark force that controlled her.

Yipes reached for the knife and Matilda lurched out of the chair and slashed, cutting deeply into the back of his hand. She cried out that she was sorry, and for a moment she seemed herself again. Yipes seemed not to care that his hand was bleeding. He wouldn't take his eyes off her. The space around the table was dark but for the scattered light thrown from the one lamp on the table.

"It's because of me this happened to you," Yipes said. "I should be at the bottom of the Lonely Sea, but you risked your life to save me."

"Be careful, Yipes," I whispered. "It's not just Matilda you're talking to."

"Show me, Matilda," said Yipes, undeterred. "Show me where he touched you."

Yipes was more focused on where Abaddon and Matilda had touched than he was about whether or not she would slash and mortally wound him. He was standing close enough to touch her.

"You don't need to say, just nod," he said. "Did he touch your back? Your legs? Your neck?"

She didn't respond until he said "your neck." At that, she jumped back and put the knife next to Sir Alistair's chest.

"Get away from me!" she yelled. Yipes kept moving forward, though — he would not let her go — and Matilda cried out, "Please, Yipes! Please get back! Don't come any closer!"

She was struggling between the power of love inside her and the dark presence that had invaded her mind and heart. There was nothing I could say as she held the knife close to Sir Alistair and Yipes continued to move forward, his hand steady and purposeful.

"Show me," whispered Yipes.

"I can't," said Matilda through sobs of grief and confusion. She lowered her head with the weight of all that she carried, and when she did, Yipes put his arm out quickly and touched the long hair that covered the back of her neck.

"Don't make me do this, Yipes," said Matilda, raising her head and pointing the knife toward his stomach.

"It's over now — you can stop worrying so much," Yipes replied. And with that he jerked his arm away from Matilda's neck fast and hard. Matilda threw her head back and screamed in pain, raising the knife as if to strike. But then she went unexpectedly limp, falling backward into Yipes's arms. She appeared to have fainted dead away.

"What did you do?" Marco and I both asked as we came forward and helped lay her down on the smooth stone floor of the chamber.

Yipes carefully took his hand from behind her head.

"Yipes, you've killed her!" I cried. His hand was quite literally covered in blood.

"Don't be ridiculous. Of course I didn't kill her."

He wiped the blood away and I realized how stupid I'd been — it was his injured hand, dripping blood all over everything.

"Here's the problem," said Yipes. He smeared the blood free from his fingertips and there, held in his little hand, was a rusted metal shard.

"Is that — ?" I began to ask.

"A scale from Abaddon's arm? I believe it is. It was hidden all the while behind all that beautiful hair of hers. But it's out now. She's going to be fine."

"Nicely done," said Sir Alistair. We all looked at once to see that he was very much awake and in good spirits. "I was getting tired of being all tied up."

I turned back and saw that Matilda had come awake as well.

"Yipes," I said.

"What?"

I nodded toward Matilda and he saw her.

"What's happened?" she asked. She didn't look to me or Marco or Sir Alistair — only Yipes.

"Nothing much," said Yipes, carefully placing Abaddon's scale in his vest pocket. "We flew *Stargazer* around and tied up Sir Alistair for fun. You've been sleeping."

"Sleeping? No, I remember — he made me . . ."

"It's all right, Matilda. You're not going to be bothered anymore," I said.

She sat up and turned toward Sir Alistair. "I'm terrible!" she cried. "I hit poor old Alistair over the head with the biggest rock I could find. And you" — she turned back toward me — "I almost killed you more than once and let Marco take the blame."

Marco had been completely vindicated — and yet he didn't gloat or make a fuss. He was genuinely pleased to have found his place within a band of friends he could trust.

"You four will make a very good team," said Sir Alistair, wriggling uncomfortably against the ropes that held him to the chair. "Could someone release me?"

We were all embarrassed for having left him tied up.

"Of course," said Yipes, holding the knife out to Matilda. "Why not do the honor?"

"But I can't be trusted. I can't even begin to say how sorry —"

Yipes put his other hand up — the one that really needed a bandage — and stopped Matilda from trying to do any more explaining.

"There's nothing to forgive. It wasn't you doing those things. Now please, cut the ropes, and let's get back to work. We've got to get out of here."

Matilda looked at each and every one of us and knew

that we not only didn't feel a need to judge her, we also trusted her. As she began cutting the ropes that held Sir Alistair, there was a crashing sound from below and the fourth stone pillar wobbled ever so slightly.

"Someone's awake," I said. "We'd better hurry."

CHAPTER 21

DAWN BREAKS ⊙N THE FIVE STONE PILLARS

"The sun will begin to rise within the hour."

Sir Alistair was standing at the edge of the chamber, looking out at the fading darkness. He had grown faint of spirit as the night wore on, shuffling around the chamber more and more slowly.

"Do you think it will be that soon?" I asked.

"I'm certain of it."

He hobbled to a table and checked something that looked like an extra-large compass. Then he touched a weather dial of sorts and scanned some torn charts and maps. "We best keep at our preparations. Sleep will have to wait."

I was exhausted from all our preparations and the long previous day, but I'd known this sort of need for stamina before. My body had gotten used to what I sometimes needed to put it through, as if it had a storehouse of several extra days and I could call on them when I really needed to. The only problem was that sleep would have to come eventually, and when it did, it would be long and deep.

"Help me pack these things away, Alexa," Sir Alistair continued. "You're going to need them."

Sir Alistair and I went slowly back and forth between his tables full of gadgets and the giant box under *Stargazer*. He explained each item to me as we went — some of which defied my understanding — and I nodded continuously, trying to take it all in. There were journals full of drawings, which I aimed to explore when I had more time. And there were delicate tools, slide rules and an abacus, yellowed paper in bundles, a wooden box filled with magnifying glasses, inkwells, old pens, droppers, and tweezers.

"We've packed up all the food and containers of saltwater and drinking water," Yipes came alongside to report, something he'd been doing every now and then for several hours.

"What about your hand — how's it doing?" I asked. "Will you be able to assume all your duties once we get *Stargazer* airborne again?"

"Good as new!" Yipes answered, holding his injured hand so that we could see it. "Matilda wrapped it up nicely."

"How's she doing? Is she . . . herself?"

"She's still feeling the sting of guilt, but she's doing better. She's also worried about Ranger. This is the longest he's ever been apart from her. "

I hadn't ever had a pet of my own, unless I could count Murphy. Murphy was a wild squirrel looking for adventure, but it was hard to think of him as a pet.

"We'll get her back home come morning," said Sir

Alistair. "For now, we need to finish things up and pre-pare to take off. This might not go as you expect."

"What do you mean?" I asked.

"Trust me. Nothing like this ever goes exactly as planned."

Sir Alistair was right. I'd been in many scuffles over the past two years, and they always ended up surprising me in the end. I wondered how my journey from the Five Stone Pillars would turn out differently than I'd expected. It was best to be alert and prepared for anything.

"Load the last of the things," Sir Alistair instructed, "including the animals. I'm going to let the fish go."

"How are you going to do that?" asked Yipes.

Sir Alistair looked at Yipes inquisitively, as if he'd asked a dull question.

"Pull the plugs, of course."

"Can I help?" I asked, enthusiastic about the idea of releasing a hammerhead shark, a giant squid, and a lot of other creatures of the sea back to their home.

Yipes went one direction to look for Grump and the cats, and to get an update from Marco on the blankets and pillows he was gathering. One thing about a wooden box — it's hard. The blankets and pillows would help the children sleep and keep them warm if we happened to start off on a long expedition.

When we arrived at the tanks, I asked Sir Alistair how he'd gotten the fish inside in the first place.

"They're easy to catch when they're little," he replied.

"So these have all grown up in captivity. I hope they'll do all right in the depths of the Lonely Sea."

With that, he released a lever at the side of the first of six tanks. There was a sound of popping and gurgling as the water swooshed through a large hole in the bottom and all the fish disappeared into the floor. The weird brilliance of Sir Alistair Wakefield never ceased to amaze me.

"But where did they go?" I asked.

"Down through the middle of the pillar some distance, then *zing!* into the open air and down into the water."

"Sounds fun," I said with some sarcasm. I didn't imagine it would feel very good to flip and flop through the air only to smack into the ocean below. All the tanks were emptied without difficulty, except for an octopus that wouldn't let go of the side. It held on with all eight arms while its head dangled into the hole and water shot past. It wasn't until a giant tuna came barreling through that the suction cups finally succumbed and the octopus disappeared for good.

"Only one thing left to do," said Sir Alistair.

"What's that?" I asked. It appeared that we'd packed all the important things we needed and the sun was about to come up.

"A few personal items I need to gather from my room."

I realized I hadn't seen Sir Alistair's room. I didn't even know he had one. I got the feeling he wanted a few minutes alone, so I let him go alone toward the models of the Wakefield House and the Five Stone Pillars. To my bewilderment, he stooped down low at the door to the Wakefield House and disappeared inside.

"What a strange man," I said aloud. "All this space and he chooses the cramped quarters of the Wakefield House to make his home."

With Sir Alistair occupied and all of our preparations complete, I looked skyward at the model of the Five Stone Pillars. The towering fifth pillar stood high above the rest. In fact, it was so high the top ended in darkness, somewhere near the ceiling of the chamber.

"I wonder . . ."

There were catwalks all through the open space. Some cut across the middle and others ran around the edges. Looking up into the dim torches that lit the walls, I saw that one of the bridges led high on the ledge to a perch that would look right down on the top of the model of the fifth pillar. With the little time I had left, I decided I would climb up there and see what I could see.

I made the first few switchbacks up the side of the wall without carrying a torch, but when it became darker the higher I went, I took one of the torches from its holder against the stone wall before going on.

"It's colder up here," I said to myself. "And a little wet."

The walls of the chamber began to curve in ever so slightly. They were moist and chilly as I touched them to keep my balance. I came to a point where I could look down on all but the fifth pillar. It was magnificent even in the faint torchlight. They were quite detailed, showing the first with fields of grain and orchards, the lake at the center of the second pillar with trees and houses scattered all around. The third pillar had vines running all through its concave surface, just like the real skimming pillar, and the fourth was round and green on top. Sir Alistair could really make a model.

I also saw all that was below me from my high perch. The vast presence of *Stargazer* stood unmoving and solid as it waited to escape into the open. The Wakefield House model, the empty tanks, Yipes walking with Grump across the floor of the chamber. And something else, something not so good.

"Uh-oh," I said out loud. The light was beginning to dance on the distant water. Dawn was coming fast.

I looked up — only a little way to go. There was no sound from below of Abaddon making his final assault, so I quickly made my way to the very top and leaned out over the rail.

"You've got to be kidding me," I said. There was only one thing on the top of the model, hidden behind the walls that rose up around the edges. It was a tree, twisted down at its center to look like — could it be? — a question mark.

"Maybe there are some things even Sir Alistair doesn't know."

I turned to start down the long catwalk just in time to hear Abaddon smashing into the pillar below. This time the fourth pillar shook harder and longer than I'd felt it shake before. The ceiling rained with dirt and tiny pebbles, and I watched in horror as the bridge I walked on began to wobble back and forth.

"Yipes!" I hollered, dropping the torch over the edge and holding on to the trembling rail.

"What's she doing up there?" I heard Marco say from below.

"I haven't the slightest idea," cried Yipes. The two of them were swiftly racing toward me as I descended one step at a time.

I thought I'd gotten rid of you!

It was the voice of Abaddon, violent with renewed rage. The sound of the pillar being destroyed below grew louder and the inside of the chamber rumbled loudly.

"Get *Stargazer* airborne!" I cried. "We've got to get it out of here before the whole chamber comes crashing down!"

"We're not leaving without you," yelled Matilda. Then, looking around, she added, "Where's Sir Alistair?"

"In the Wakefield House," I shouted. But I was determined to get them moving as I advanced into a run on the catwalk. "I'm going to make it — I'll get Sir Alistair. You three gather the cats and Grump and get *Stargazer* flying! That's an order!"

I'd never spoken with such authority before, and the three of them seemed to understand that the captain meant business. They scurried back toward *Stargazer* and began to let the anchor lines go. Yipes ran right behind Grump and squeezed him through the sliding door of the box.

As I neared the bottom, the rumbling grew more intense and I heard a sound from above. The top of the Wakefield House was crumbling loose. I knew from the story Roland had told me that if the model was anything like the real thing, the Wakefield House was about to tumble over into a thousand pieces.

"Sir Alistair! Get out!" I cried, reaching the bottom and going to the door. I took a deep breath, then darted through. I found him sitting at a little table with a lamp, reading a book.

"Get up, Sir Alistair! We have to go!"

I grabbed him by the arm and he glanced up at me with those ancient eyes of his

"I'll only slow you down," said Sir Alistair. "I think the moment of my passing has finally come."

The light from the lamp danced in his eyes as he closed the book.

"Take this with you," he said. "All the secrets of my long life are hidden inside."

"I'd rather take you," I said. With a strength I didn't know I had, I lifted him by the shoulder against his will and dragged him toward the door. He let the book slip from his fingers and reached back for it, but I didn't care about the book. The Wakefield House was coming down.

"Leave it behind!" I said, hauling Sir Alistair out into the open of the chamber. My crew had done well. They had *Stargazer* out in the open, held only by the one long rope wound into the pulley.

All at once, the sun was on the water and dawn had come. The chamber quaked and rocked wildly back and forth as the Wakefield House tumbled to the ground. Catwalks and rope bridges tangled and snapped in the air, wrapping their long arms around the falling structure until the twisted wreckage hit the floor and everything shattered into pieces.

Sir Alistair cried out and stumbled to the ground. I could no longer hold him up.

"My back," he whispered through clenched teeth. "I've been struck."

A flying boulder, a piece of wood — I didn't know what had hit him or how hard, but I wasn't going to let him die alone in the crumbling chamber.

"Get up!" I screamed, putting my shoulder under his arm and hauling him up under the one remaining rope. "You can do this if you try."

Matilda flung her slider into the air before I could cry out for help. It skidded and landed at my feet. I gave Sir Alistair the slider and put one of the knots in each of his crooked old hands.

"Hold on tight and don't let go for anything," I commanded.

Sir Alistair winced in pain but held firm.

"Yipes!" I cried, facing *Stargazer* where she waited out in the open air. "Throw me a vine!"

Yipes did as I instructed and I tied the vine around Sir Alistair's waist. All the while, the ceiling of the chamber continued to crumble, sheets of rock falling from the sky, knocking down pillars and tables and tanks. The sound was deafening.

"PULL!" I screamed. "Pull as fast as you can!"

Marco left his post at the controls and heaved with Yipes.

"Sir Alistair, hold on. Don't let go!" I instructed again.

The pressure on his back as the rope began to drag him out over the edge into the open air seemed to take his breath away, but he held on as Marco and Yipes towed him up and into the box.

"We've got him! We've got him!" cried Matilda.

"Throw back the slider!" I yelled. Matilda hurled the slider across the open space between us and it skidded across the chamber floor a few feet off. Hanging bridges were tumbling in snarled heaps to the floor of the chamber as I crawled toward the knotted piece of rope that was my only means of escape. I couldn't hear anything but the sound of devastation, until through the violence that surrounded me there came a voice of fire and might.

You think your friends are freed, but they will perish the same as you.

"You can't control Matilda any longer. I would have expected you to know that in all your vast knowledge."

Sometimes you just know something is happening without hearing it or seeing it, and I absolutely knew that Abaddon was trying to bring Matilda under his control in the devastation that surrounded me. He was telling her to throw Yipes overboard or cut the ropes to the balloon with a hidden knife, *anything* that would prevent our escape. I had a moment of halfhearted contentment because I knew she wouldn't hear him now or ever again. Abaddon's voice was left to me alone.

My moment of bliss was to be brief indeed, for the moment Abaddon knew he'd been dealt an unexpected blow, he flew into an even greater frenzy. I knew it would be his final assault. He wouldn't stop until the work of bringing the fourth pillar crashing into the Lonely Sea was completed.

The rim of the opening to the outside began to shake and crumble and I scurried farther back from the edge. A colossal stone broke free and fell from the ceiling and I watched it as if in slow motion. In its path was the rope that held *Stargazer*, and when it hit, the box holding my friends pitched severely into the air. Yipes nearly flew free from the rope he held and Matilda slammed hard into the side of the box. When the rope snapped in two, *Stargazer*'s box careened out of control. My flying ship was free to go without me. Bobbing back and forth, the box began to rise as giant stones rained down.

I see that you are trapped. I'm only disappointed you won't be here to see what plans I have for this place!

I watched as Marco dove headfirst over the back side of *Stargazer*. In his arms, he held a long, thin vine and he free-fell for thirty feet or more. When the vine caught his weight, it stretched thinner still, and he snapped hard and fast toward the opening of the chamber. It would be close — so close that I would have to leave the chamber to meet him.

I stood and ran. I didn't try to dodge the falling sky around me. I just ran as fast as my legs would carry me and I called on Elyon to make my path straight and true. When I reached the very end of the chamber, I jumped into the air with all the strength I had left. Marco was there, holding out one hand, and I slammed into him. There was no hesitation in his aim to save me, and I found his strong arm holding me firmly as we drifted back under *Stargazer*.

I looked at him then as I hadn't looked at him before, with something from deeper inside.

"Thank you." It was all I could think to say as we stared at each other. It felt like the whole world had fallen away. There was only us two and nothing else.

"You're really going to owe me after this one," he said, flashing his dry smile as Yipes and Matilda hauled up the rope. *Stargazer* was rising fast, as if she'd finally been given the freedom to ride the sky.

"How's she doing?" I asked Marco, gazing up toward the balloon. "That was quite a hit she took."

"You and this contraption were made for each other — both tough as stone . . . but, I don't know, gentle at the same time."

"Are you being . . . what is it . . . *nice* to me?" I asked.

Marco didn't answer, and as we rose higher into the air, we both fell quiet, realizing that the world of the Five Stone Pillars was about to be changed forever.

CHAPTER 22
THE FIFTH PILLAR

Abaddon continued his assault on the fourth pillar. I was safely at the helm of *Stargazer* and Marco was seated at the pedals, guiding us away from the destruction. Yipes stood on the rim of the box, holding tight to a rope and watching with great interest as the fourth pillar continued to wobble and shake. Matilda trimmed the heated air from the tube at my request, and then we all waited for what would happen next.

"This will be interesting," said Sir Alistair, sitting wearily on one of the long benches in the box. "I don't think it will come to pass as you believe."

"What do you mean?" asked Yipes. "What's going to happen?"

We all speculated and argued back and forth about what was to come next, but Sir Alistair would only repeat one thing over and over again: "Take us higher. Higher still."

And so we did. Matilda opened up the tube and we rose higher on the heated air between the fourth and the fifth pillar.

"It's going to fall," said Yipes, pointing down to the fourth pillar. "It's really wobbling now."

"Look there," said Matilda. There was something unexpected in her voice — a new kind of surprise. She had moved to the other side of the box and was staring at the fifth pillar. We had come all the way up, even with the walls that towered around the top. I was reminded again of Bridewell and how my adventures had begun when I'd overcome walls of stone and ventured outside. But things were different now. I didn't want to know what was outside these walls. I wanted to know what was *inside*. I had come full circle in a sense, and there was something true and perfect as we rose above the walls of the fifth pillar and saw what lay hidden.

"You see there," said Sir Alistair. "I still have a few tricks up my sleeve."

Everything happened at once then, and I saw the whole thing from the best seat in the house — high in the air, riding *Stargazer* over a scene I will never forget. It began when the fourth pillar tipped slowly toward the third pillar and everyone but Sir Alistair groaned with horror at what was about to occur. Abaddon had moved off beneath the fifth pillar to await the very end, his snakelike arms slapping against the water as he howled with dark pleasure.

At the very same moment when it seemed the third pillar was doomed to be struck by the force of its once peaceful neighbor, something unexpected and wonderful was set into motion. The chamber we'd escaped was three quarters of the way up the fourth stone pillar and it was a vast, open space within an otherwise solid structure. The top third broke free, crashing down into the rest of the pillar. It was a vast amount of weight and force on the side of the pillar Abaddon left alone, and it brought the fourth pillar tipping in a different direction than Abaddon had intended. It was now on a collision course with the fifth pillar, the tallest of them all.

The fourth pillar swayed and, gaining speed, struck the fifth pillar right in its middle. The sound was explosive and enormous, the kind of sound that makes you put your hands over your ears and takes your breath away. The fifth pillar wobbled and cracked, and then the entire top half tipped and fell toward the Lonely Sea and the beast that waited there.

What we had seen beyond the walls of the fifth pillar was now headed toward our enemy. As the top of the pillar turned to fall, we all marveled at the forest of stone spikes that covered its top. It had looked something like a great plain of standing trees, stripped bare of all but the shooting trunks. But these trees were not of wood, they were of stone, hundreds of feet long and heading straight for the sea monster that raged below.

This cannot be so.

"Oh, but it is," I whispered. "He has made this to defeat you."

Abaddon dove for the bottom of the Lonely Sea as the top of the fifth stone pillar plummeted. The scene was at once marvelous and terrifying. An object heavy and huge beyond imagining, falling through morning mist — the air full with the sound of crashing. *Stargazer* was brushed back by the violent wind of two immense forces colliding into each other — one of stone and one of water — and we all held tight as the box rocked back and forth. Waves rose on the sea and millions of tiny droplets shot into the air. I was amazed to see the Lonely Sea was not so deep here as I'd imagined. The fifth stone pillar slowed suddenly about halfway down, clearly hitting bottom and sticking well out of the water. In the wake around its edges, there grew a black cloud of blood and shards of metal. Abaddon was crushed, stuck with a thousand stone arrows at the bottom of the Lonely Sea.

And then I heard a sound that made my heart skip a beat. It was soft and faraway, but it was also strikingly clear. Looking off toward the three pillars that remained, I caught a distant glimpse of people cheering.

"Is everyone all right?" I asked, though I knew from the smiles and howls of laughter that my crew was doing just fine. Yipes swung all the way around one of the vines to the balloon and let go, landing on the long platform where Sir Alistair sat quietly smiling. They were eye to eye — Yipes really was *that* short — and Yipes raised one eyebrow at the oldest man in the world.

"Did you know about this?"

Sir Alistair only shrugged.

"You're a crafty one," said Yipes, twisting the end of his long mustache.

"You don't know the half of it," said Sir Alistair, laughing ever so lightly and flinching once again at the pain he was trying so hard to hide.

"We better get you back on land," I said. Pointing toward the sound of cheering people, I directed Marco to begin pedaling and aim *Stargazer* for the first pillar.

"The fields of wheat will be a perfect place to land," I said. "Lots of open, flat space — just what *Stargazer* needs."

Everyone nodded their agreement as Marco began pedaling fast, guiding us with the rudders over the top of the third pillar. I leaned over and waved, crying out to everyone below to race as fast as they could to the first pillar and meet us there. We were close enough to see clearer now as we descended slowly on our path. I saw Jonezy waving with everyone else, and Phylo running down the hill on his way to the bridges that would lead him to our landing space. He wanted to be there first, and it looked as if he would get his wish. There were a great many hands held over mouths and fingers pointing as we sailed over. *Stargazer* was a sight they were having a hard time believing.

We passed slowly across the third pillar, which had never looked so mysterious and beautiful. The crossing vines, I now saw from above, were set in a pattern like the weave of a blanket. The sun danced on the vines and turned them different shades of brown against the lavish green floor of the pillar. When we came to the gap between the third and the second pillar, we were lower still and I heard the distinct sound of barking from more than one dog. All the dogs were staring up at us, loud with excitement, and none was more excited than Ranger as Matilda leaned over and yelled his name.

"Good boy!" she cried. She took her slider from her belt and threw it overboard into the blue lake at the center of the second pillar. Ranger watched the slider tumble end over end through the air and hit with a splash.

"Go get it!" Matilda yelled. Ranger was off in a flash at his master's command, racing for the slider floating somewhere in the lake.

"No more hot air," I said as we reached the gap between the first and second pillars. We had already trimmed the air in the tube back to almost nothing, but now, with it shut entirely, we began to lose altitude more quickly. Looking down, I saw Phylo making his way across the rope bridge on his way to the first pillar.

"Phylo!" cried Matilda. "Will you set a barrel and bring Ranger over with you?"

Phylo was nothing if not a helpful boy, and he turned back from where he'd come to find Ranger wet and waiting with the slider in his mouth. He called him safely into a basket and moved it on its vines over the open air, holding the lead rope as he'd been taught. When he started over the bridge again, he was pulling Ranger alongside, and he was still ahead of everyone else, but only just barely. People streamed in behind him. The rope bridge wobbled and swayed on the weight of so many, but no one seemed to mind in the least. They'd lived this way their entire lives, and though it seemed perilous to me, I had to imagine it was like a walk in a park for them. We were well above on our approach and would need to circle, letting the balloon glide down as the hot air grew cooler inside the gigantic balloon.

As Marco pulled hard on the right rudder, we began a slow, circling descent to the wheat field below.

"I wonder if this thing could hold Armon," asked Yipes, looping a long rope over and over around his arm. "He'd be a heavy load."

Sir Alistair liked to solve problems. Glancing back and forth at the space around him, he began to calculate things in his mind.

"The balloon could carry him," Sir Alistair said at length. "But there wouldn't be any room for a crew."

Yipes snorted, amused by the idea of a giant in the box, sitting as he once had in the clock tower at the City of Dogs with his knees pulled up to his chin.

Yipes tossed the first rope out, then another that was coiled in the box at the other side, then another and another. Soon there were four ropes held at each corner by the strongest of the men below. I guided their movements from my seat. We landed gently on the soft bed of growing green wheat, which was smashed to the ground under the weight of the box.

Everyone gathered near, gazing up at the balloon and

calling our names with great excitement. Ranger pranced up beside the box and Matilda wrapped her arms around the wet dog. Midnight and Nimbus stayed on board and everyone marveled at the sight of the mysterious-looking black cats. Grump was asleep under one of the long platforms until Phylo found him and cried, "Wow! Look at this!"

And, of course, everyone looked on in utter amazement at the sight of Sir Alistair Wakefield, who sat unmoving, gazing out over the many lost children from The Land of Elyon.

"It's time *Stargazer* brought some of us home," he said with a weak but meaningful smile. "Prepare for our departure when morning comes again."

That was the full extent of what Sir Alistair said that day. He looked upon the people and the remaining pillars and nodded softly, then lay down in the box and wouldn't speak anything more.

He left everything else to me.

CHAPTER 23

OUR DEPARTURE

Midnight and Nimbus tucked in close to Sir Alistair, purring softly and keeping him company. Grump also stayed in the box and seemed perfectly content to sleep the entire morning away.

"He's not going to make it," said Jonezy as we veered off and talked privately. Everyone was standing amid the wheat. They had pushed down a big swath around *Stargazer* so that we could all stand together on the first pillar.

"I think you might be right," I offered. "He's so old and fragile. Maybe it's finally his time to go after all these years."

"What should we do?" asked Jonezy. "He won't leave that contraption of his. It's as if he's expected somewhere and he doesn't want to miss the ride."

I had been thinking about just that for some time.

"I think I know where he wants to go."

Jonezy looked at me curiously and then nodded. He had come to trust me in the stir of all that had happened.

"When Warvolds are about, things always tend to end well."

It was sometimes hard to think of myself as Thomas

Warvold's daughter or as Roland Warvold's niece. It always felt like a lot to live up to. I turned where I stood and found that everyone was staring at me, wondering what I was going to do next. I didn't make them wait, because I felt time was precious.

"It was an accident, my bringing that monster to the foot of the Five Stone Pillars. But it's gone now. It will never bother you again."

The news was met with a flurry of cheers.

"This place is hidden from the dangers of the world. But, as you've seen, even hidden places can be found and threatened. This strange vessel — this *airship* — was made for two reasons. The first is to continue caring for all who live here. I believe I can sail it between this secret place and The Land of Elyon. I can bring you what you need — clothing, seeds, tools — and I can make the trip often. The winds change directions like clockwork. They will drive me away and draw me near as need requires."

"What's the second reason for *Stargazer?*" asked Phylo. He had a big grin on his face. He knew what the reason was, but he wanted to hear it from me.

"For those who want to go back home — either to visit or to stay — *Stargazer* is for you."

Phylo was so excited he leaped into the air and ran for the balloon. "I'm first! I'm first!"

I hadn't thought to ask, but Jonezy leaned over and whispered that Phylo was one of the very last lost children brought to the Five Stone Pillars. His father had been killed by Grindall and the ogres, but rumor had it that his mother lived on in Castalia.

"The wind draws us away on this very morning," I said, for I decided not to wait another day. Sir Alistair was nearing the end of his life, the wind was up, and I was itching to put *Stargazer* through her paces on a long voyage. "But I can't take any of you with me just yet."

"I'm going!" cried Phylo. He had wrapped his arms around a vine holding *Stargazer* to the ground, and it didn't look like he was going to let go without a fight.

"We don't know exactly how it will work," I continued. "Only Yipes and I — along with a small crew — are to leave off on this first journey."

I wasn't sure if Marco would be willing to go along with me and discover the world outside the Five Stone Pillars to test *Stargazer*'s worthiness. But I needed only to look at him standing beside the box and I knew in an instant that he, too, had found a greater purpose in life. He would be a lifeline between two places and I felt a certainty he would stay on with me.

Matilda was a different matter. I had known the feeling of having an older sister for the first time in my life and I was about to have something else in common with Roland and Thomas. Just as they had known they needed to go separate ways, I knew I had to leave Matilda behind.

"My place is here," she said.

I nodded, knowing she was right.

"I'll take her place!" yelled Phylo from where he held the vine. "I can do it!"

I looked at Jonezy and shrugged. Phylo was a very able child and his duties would be light. It could work.

"Fine," I said with a sternness in my voice. "You can come along, but you'll have plenty of work to do. This isn't a vacation."

Phylo beamed with excitement and ran off to pack his things, yelling over his shoulder that he would pelt us with rocks if we tried to leave without him.

Yipes had been fidgeting with his hat and his mustache as he stood off to the side of me, nervously listening to every word. He walked up to Matilda and the two of them stood together, both of them only a foot higher than Ranger's head. Ranger was in a friendly mood and licked persistently at Yipes's cheek until Matilda told him to lie down.

"I have to go . . . well, I think I should . . . I need to, um, go away now," said Yipes. He was a real stumbler with his words when he was nervous — and he was *really* nervous.

"I know," said Matilda. "It's okay."

Yipes was squeezing and twisting his hat so hard it was crumpling in his hands.

"I was, um, wondering," he stammered. "If, you know, when I came back . . ."

"Oh, just ask her already!" cried Marco. "We're all waiting."

Yipes bent down on one knee, which made Ranger think he wanted to play. There was a lot of licking and barking before Yipes stood back up and took Matilda's hand in his.

"What I wanted to ask was . . ." He seemed to calm down at the look in her eyes, and then finally he asked.

"Would you . . . would you marry me?"

Matilda began to cry, but she was able to answer him.

"Yes, Yipes. I'll marry you when you come back."

Yipes threw his hat high into the air and the two embraced while everyone clapped and congratulated them. I think they might have hugged all day if Ranger hadn't returned with the hat, nudging his nose between them and begging for attention.

"How long will it take for you to return?" Matilda asked.

Yipes glanced at me and I, in turn, looked toward the box where Sir Alistair had sat up with a smile. He sniffed at the wind and offered his best guess.

"It will be at least two weeks there, but we've chosen our time well. She'll be able to turn back straight away. I think *Stargazer* can have him back in a month's time, six weeks at the outside."

"That will give us time to plan the wedding!" cried the girls who had befriended me at the first skim. They laughed and clapped, electrified by the idea of planning the event.

"Can you do it at night, on the third pillar?" I said,

for though it wasn't my wedding, I had an idea of how magical it could be. "And can we include a night skim in the celebration?"

"I think that would be perfect," said Matilda.

Yipes kissed her hand. Matilda laughed at the feel of his fuzzy mustache, and when Yipes turned to look at me, I could see that for the first time in his life he was at peace with who he was and where he was going. "It's settled then," said Jonezy. "Alexa and her team will make the maiden voyage alone. Upon her return, you will all have to decide if and when you want to go back to The Land of Elyon. If you do choose to go, you'll have to decide whether you'll ever want to come back. Alexa, how many can you carry at once, do you think?"

I turned to Sir Alistair, but he was resting again.

"I think it would be safest to carry no more than ten on our first voyages. But if things work like I hope they will, we can make four or five round-trips a year. If you want to go, you'll be able to go; it will only be a matter of when."

"We'll have it all worked out on your return — don't you worry."

There were murmurs of "I want to go" and "I'm not leaving" and "Can I visit and come back?" as everyone began thinking of their futures.

"And what about him?" Matilda asked softly, pointing to where Sir Alistair appeared to be sleeping.

I only paused a moment before answering.

"He's going with us."

I knew where Sir Alistair Wakefield needed to go. It was only a matter of whether I could take him there or not.

"What about *that*?" asked Jonezy. "And those?"

He had pointed to Grump, who was at that very moment loping out into the wheat field looking for something to eat. Midnight and Nimbus both sat on his back. Seeing that I was watching, Midnight bounded in my direction. I leaned down to hear her.

"We've decided to stay," she said, quiet and close to my ear. "All three of us. We don't want to be separated."

After some discussion of what would be best for everyone involved, it was decided that Grump, Midnight, and Nimbus would be left on the second pillar in the care of Jonezy and Matilda. Before morning turned to afternoon, we had moved *Stargazer* to the shore of the lake, left the animals there, and loaded the box with more provisions at the insistence of Jonezy and Matilda. Grump took naturally to a life of lying in the sun by the lake and the cats were having a heyday tormenting the dogs as we lifted off for our maiden voyage. The cats meowed, but I couldn't understand them any longer. The magic had already drifted away, somewhere out into the Lonely Sea to be caught again by a place I had yet to find.

Everyone waved at *Stargazer*'s launch, clapping and wishing us well. Sir Alistair slept along one of the benches. Marco was at the pedals, chewing on a loaf of bread and guzzling water. Yipes was teaching Phylo how to turn up the heat at the tube with powder and saltwater.

"We'll be back as fast as the wind will carry us," I yelled to the gathered crowd below.

"And I'll bring back a ring!" cried Yipes. Everyone laughed and we went higher still, until we were so high I could see all the pillars once more.

It all looked familiar and yet very different than it once did. The three pillars where everyone lived had a powerful sense of having remained the same, but everything else had changed. The fifth pillar, once so tall and mysterious, was now two shorter pillars. The half that had been the top tilted slightly to the side. Both parts seemed to have no purpose, though we all knew what a grand part they had played.

"Sir Alistair, are you awake?" I asked. He stirred and opened his eyes, still bright against a deeply weathered face. He looked old — older than time itself — but he managed to sit up and hold my hand.

"We're leaving," I said.

Yipes came close and helped steady Sir Alistair as he stood up. Looking down at what remained of the fourth pillar, he saw that it was only a bump on the water. The rest was gone.

"All my secrets are buried at sea," he said solemnly. No one spoke, and I was left with my own thoughts of what might have been hidden away on the fourth pillar if only we'd had time to discover more.

"And the way of yesterday," said Yipes. "Is that lost forever as well?"

Sir Alistair sat back down and sighed deeply.

"One might find it if he or she looked hard enough. But all who knew the way have passed on."

"You're still here," said Yipes, trying to bolster the old man's spirits. "You could find it again."

Sir Alistair didn't respond. He lay back down and was instantly asleep. It was as if all the years had piled up and were pushing against the very end of his life, making him very, very tired all at once.

"We could fly over Mount Laythen — we could find the way of yesterday and bring him home," said Yipes.

"I don't think that's where we're supposed to take him," I said. Yipes looked at me questioningly, but I was content to keep my thoughts to myself until we were closer to The Land of Elyon.

"I hope the winds are strong," I said, gazing up into a blue sky. "We need to get him home."

CHAPTER 24

A GIANT AT THE GATES

I had many thoughts on our seventeen-day journey over water. There was something magnificent about finding my way in the world, of being given a task to which I was perfectly suited. I had to imagine this was the dream of every good person — to find the world in need of the thing you love doing. It's the kind of revelation that can settle even the most adventurous heart.

All my life I'd felt a stirring to move out beyond the boundaries that held me in check. The walls of Bridewell, the Valley of Thorns, the Five Stone Pillars, the Lonely Sea — so many places that seemed at once to summon and ensnare me. It had been a long struggle between my own daring spirit and the dreaded feeling of a restless soul unable to find comfort in a place I could call home.

But those seventeen days over the water changed me forever. Finally, mercifully, my heart was at rest. I had found a purpose I could embrace. And I had found these things within the stirring of my own desire to run free over the vast expanse of the world.

Marco and I talked for hours and hours on end, often after we'd settled to float on the Lonely Sea for the night and everyone else had gone to sleep. He and I drifted closer together as Yipes took Phylo under his wing, teaching him everything from tying knots to netting fish. Sir Alistair Wakefield grew weaker with each passing day. He slept, waking only to glance at the maps, offer a small suggestion, or drink a cup of water and nibble on whatever we'd prepared to eat. There were windy days and moments of concern, long afternoons of playing games and watching the horizon, and a good deal of laughter.

On the morning of the seventeenth day, The Land of Elyon came into view, a massive pile of stone against the endless span of the Lonely Sea. By midday we were over Castalia and the City of Dogs, bringing *Stargazer* to rest beside the pile of rocks that had once been Grindall's Dark Tower. The looks on faces — especially those we knew — as we came in on Sir Alistair Wakefield's flying machine were priceless. When we landed, Yipes went straight to our old friend Balmoral and told him of the wedding.

"I have just the thing for it," I heard Balmoral say, and he pulled a chain from inside his shirt. There hung the ring his departed wife had worn, and though Yipes resisted, Balmoral refused to take no for an answer.

Seeing Phylo lifted off the ground and held by his mother was a sight to behold, one I imagined seeing many more times in the months and years to come as I traversed the Lonely Sea. We were able to share the wonderful news that this would not be our last visit. We would be bringing children home soon enough.

"We can't stay on," I said after an all-too-brief encounter with old and new friends. "But we'll be back. Watch the horizon for our return."

There was a profound sadness at our leaving so suddenly, and a great many questions I tried to answer as best I could. When would we return? Who would we bring with us? Could anyone come along? Why couldn't we stay? And so much more. But we simply had to go.

When we were airborne once more, Sir Alistair stirred, as if he were gathering the very last of what energy he had. He sat upright for the first time in many days and watched The Land of Elyon pass before his eyes. The great lake of Castalia with Mount Laythen towering to its left. The dreadful Valley of Thorns, an immovable reminder of a dark age. The Dark Hills, so vast and empty of life. The town of Bridewell, which gave us all delight when we saw it from above. We came in low over the library at Renny Lodge and called down to Grayson and Pervis Kotcher. They were utterly dumbstruck by the grand contraption we floated by in, and I promised to visit them soon. All my memories of Jocastas and animals came back to me as Marco steered us along the side of Mount Laythen and over Fenwick Forest.

"Keep going," I kept saying. "Keep going until you can go no farther."

And so he did, pedaling with all his might as we made our way over the Sly Field and into the mist that lay in front of the Tenth City. I turned to Sir Alistair, who remained weary and yet almost childlike with wonder.

"Go a little more," I said, the mist so thick we couldn't see two feet on any side of *Stargazer*.

"I know this place, though I've never been here," Sir Alistair said.

I could see him smiling through the misty air. We had come to a place even he couldn't imagine or create.

"Bring us down," I said, and Yipes trimmed the heated air from the tube. The mist lay heavy with chill, and *Stargazer* responded by drifting quickly toward the ground. As we neared the bottom, the mist began to clear and we saw the ground advancing below. After that, it was as if Elyon himself had taken control of *Stargazer*, so gentle was our approach. We needed no ropes or anchors as we landed on a soft, grassy field spotted with trees and glistening paths lined with shimmering color.

I looked into Sir Alistair Wakefield's ancient eyes.

"You're home," I said. The parting mist revealed magnificent gates of intricate gold that marked the entrance to the Tenth City.

"I've been waiting around so long," said Sir Alistair. "I thought maybe I'd been forgotten."

A figure came into view, walking up a winding path toward the gate as it swung open. I felt my time was short, but I wanted to honor Sir Alistair Wakefield for all he'd done over his hundreds of years of service. He was the very last part of a noble past.

"You've done well," I stammered, unable to think of how to even begin to thank him. We all looked at him with watery eyes, counting the tremendous cost he'd paid on our behalf. He had ushered in the era of Thomas and Roland Warvold and had orchestrated the rescue of the lost children at a time of great peril in the world. He'd given us *Stargazer*, and I was certain that somehow, someway, it had been him all along who planned the demise of Abaddon the sea monster. And yet the three words were all I could come up with. They would have to be enough, for a looming figure approached the gate with words of his own.

"You kept everyone waiting a long time," said Armon the giant, looking and sounding more magnificent than ever. "We were beginning to wonder."

From behind Armon there came two more men — Thomas and Roland Warvold — a familiar adventurous twinkle in their eyes. It made me wonder what they'd been up to. Somewhere down the path was the silhouette of another — could it be John Christopher? — waving from afar. How I wished I could go inside with Sir Alistair, to finally make my own way back, but my time to return home hadn't arrived. There were still people with a need to be served. I only hoped I wouldn't have to wait as long as Sir Alistair had.

"Come on then," said Roland, rolling his arm as I'd

seen him do before. His memory was fresh in my mind and I wanted him to come back — I wanted them all to come back. Instead Sir Alistair stood up looking more alive than he had in weeks. He slid open the door to the box and walked out.

"He had big plans for you," I said with tears rolling down my face. "That's why it took so long."

Sir Alistair stopped and turned back, looking with affection at Marco, Yipes, and me.

"We all play our part. Some roles just drag on a little more than others."

"Tell Armon I said hello — and John Christopher, and Thomas and especially Roland, since he's only just arrived," said Yipes. He was trying to keep from getting upset, and the talking helped.

"I'll be happy to," said Sir Alistair, turning to go. The mist began filling in around *Stargazer* before he'd reached the gate, and we were left with a bleary view of three men and a giant waving as the gate closed. Sir Alistair Wakefield was finally home after all those years, and my heart sank at the thought of a world without Thomas, Roland, Sir Alistair, Armon, John Christopher — so many I'd lost along the way.

Just as I thought my heart would break, I heard a faraway voice I hadn't thought I would ever hear again.

I have many things that need doing, and so it will be awhile for you.

My breath caught in my throat.

"What is it, Alexa?" asked Marco, but I gave him no reply.

The distant sound of Elyon's voice carried on a soft wind — or it *made* the soft wind, I couldn't be sure — and *Stargazer* rocked gently back and forth.

I have something for you.

I thought the words — *What is it?* — but I couldn't speak them.

It's something I think you'll like.

Elyon's voice was the sweetest sound of all, and I no longer felt afraid of the wild world outside. I could feel him drifting away, feel the very last words coming on the wind. But I was all right now. I knew this place would be waiting for me when the time was right.

It will last until we see each other face-to-face.

Those were the last words I heard, and I didn't understand what they meant. *Until we see each other face-to-face?*

"You heard his voice again, didn't you?" asked Yipes. "You heard Elyon!"

I nodded.

"Why does he always speak to you and never me?" Yipes sounded a tad more irreverent than I thought was a very good idea this close to the gates of the Tenth City. "I think he should speak to me just once."

This request was a mistake, for the moment Yipes uttered the words, a thunderous roar swept through the mist. It was a sound with the power to level mountains. I closed my eyes and felt it rumble, long and loud through

265

all space and time. When it finally passed, I opened my eyes again to find Yipes and Marco both cowering under one of the long wooden benches.

"So that's what it sounds like," said Yipes in a shaky voice. "I think I've heard enough to last me awhile."

Stargazer began to bob up and down softly, as if she were being gently released from an invisible hand. I felt there was something new nearby — something living I couldn't quite put my finger on — and I glanced outside to the misty ground below. At first, there was nothing at all, but then I saw him. Darting close then disappearing with the swishing of a bushy tail.

"Is that you, Alexa?" came a squeaky voice from the ground. "Can it really be you?"

I have something for you. It's something I think you'll like.

Elyon's words replayed in my head. It couldn't be true — Elyon couldn't have possibly —

"Murphy!" I cried, and just as quick as I could imagine, my dear squirrel friend had scampered right up the side of the box and sat smiling on the ledge. I could understand what he was saying, and he could understand me. It was better than any gift I could have hoped for, and if Eylon's words were true, I would have this gift for my whole life. For the first time since our arrival, I was happy I wouldn't be entering the Tenth City for a long time.

"It *is* you!" he chirped, elated that we could hear each other's voices and understand the words. "I saw the balloon fly over and I just knew it — I knew it was you!"

Yipes crawled out from under the bench and stood eye to eye with Murphy.

"How's the family?"

"Very well, thank you," chirped Murphy. "Would you like to meet them?"

"What did he say?" asked Yipes. I translated, adding that he could have at least said hello first.

"Let's have a look," said Yipes, ignoring my plea for better manners.

Another adult squirrel came bounding up the side of the box followed by two more grown squirrels and — I must say these are the cutest things ever — three more wee little squirrels not half the size of Murphy. He introduced them all in order — first his wife, then the older children, then the youngest — Maggie, Milton, Muncle, Mary, Marge, and MJ (which stood for Murphy Junior).

"You've been busy, I see," said Yipes.

"Lots of time on my hands without the usual adventures," said Murphy. "Tell me everything!"

But there wasn't time for everything. No matter how badly I wanted to stay and chat the day away with Murphy, Maggie, and all the rest, Elyon seemed to be pushing us onward. We'd overstayed our visit in a sacred place and it was time for us to go.

"There's to be a wedding," I whispered conspiratorially, nodding toward Yipes. Yipes blushed and pulled out the ring he'd gotten from Balmoral in Castalia.

"Very nice!" said Murphy. "But you can't leave — where are you going?"

Yipes tapped me on the shoulder, not sure if he was interrupting.

"I need a best man . . . or best . . . animal, whatever it's called. Ask him for me, won't you?"

"You want Murphy to be your best man?" I asked.

Yipes nodded vigorously. When I turned to ask Murphy, he was already begging Maggie to go.

"How long will it take?" asked Maggie. Marge, Mary, and MJ were already pleading to go along in the tiniest voices I'd ever heard.

"It will be at least a month, maybe longer," I replied.

Maggie ran down the side of the box and the whole group of children followed.

"Don't go anywhere!" said Murphy, and then he, too, ran down the box and into the mist. I could hear them talking, but they'd gone far enough away that I couldn't tell what they were saying to each other. *Stargazer* lurched sideways and lifted a foot off the ground.

"Hurry up, Murphy!" cried Yipes. Marco had taken his seat at the pedals once more and looked on with great interest at all the commotion.

"You can understand that animal?" he asked me.

"I can!" I said with a grin. I was already plotting my next visit, how I would wander into Fenwick Forest and meet up with Ander the Forest King, the wolves Darius and Odessa — everyone!

Stargazer lifted several more feet off the ground and mist filled in beneath us so that I could no longer see how high we were going. The mist was everywhere again, thick as creamy soup, and I could feel us rising on a growing wind. Elyon wanted us away, and there was no stopping us.

"You're too late, Murphy!" I cried. It was a terrible shame, because I'd really looked forward to his company on the long day's journey across the Lonely Sea.

"Not so fast," said Yipes. He lowered a coiled vine down the side of *Stargazer* as we drifted higher into the air. The rope fell a long way and didn't hit bottom; we could only see the first few feet at it disappeared into white.

"If you're down there, grab hold!" I cried.

Suddenly we broke free of the mist over the Tenth City and I realized we'd risen well up into the sky. I was just about to give up on Murphy when looking down I saw him scampering up the long rope, smiling from ear to ear.

"Adventure, here I come!" he squeaked, diving head-long into the box. When he landed, he immediately did three backflips and howled with laughter.

"I take it she said he could come along," said Yipes.

I laughed as Murphy scampered over to Marco and sat on his lap, rose on his hind legs, and sniffed all around.

"This one hasn't had a bath for a while," said Murphy.

Marco looked on and asked with great curiosity, "What did he say? Does he like me?"

"Oh, he likes you all right," I said. "And he thinks you smell like a rose garden."

With Sir Alistair safely delivered to the Tenth City, we had finally earned a small but meaningful break from our long journey. We set our course for my home of Lathbury, where we stopped to gather provisions and visit with family and friends. But Yipes was anxious to get back to Matilda, and, truth be told, I felt more at home in the air than on the ground. After three days of sleeping, eating, convincing my parents that we were perfectly safe, and telling stories of our adventures, we were ready to return to *Stargazer* . . . with me at the helm.

CHAPTER 25

THE NIGHT WEDDING

The winds were strong on our return, and *Stargazer* managed only fourteen days from takeoff to final landing in the fields of the first pillar. I would have been happy whiling away the days skimming on the third pillar, meeting with Jonezy about who would be going along and what his needs would be, visiting the gardens on the first pillar to pluck cherry tomatoes and raspberries, and attending to *Stargazer*'s many needs at docking, but all of that would have to wait.

For three days, the wedding was the big thing on everyone's mind. For three days, we cooked and baked, decorated and rehearsed, and I tried with all my might to keep Yipes from worrying himself to death. He was calm when under certain kinds of pressure — battling ogres or giant sea monsters — but put him within a day of his own wedding and he was a nervous wreck.

We were all so happy when the moment finally arrived. It was night on the third stone pillar. Glowing lamps dangled overhead in the crisscrossing vines, and beyond those were smaller dots — the stars of a clear night. Some of the lamps glowed white, others soft green, and there was magic in the air around us. The village of

271

small homes overgrown with moss and tiny blooming flowers had been transformed into an even greater place of wonder. A long pathway was adorned with glowing emerald patterns of circles and stars. Daisies were in bloom everywhere along the twisting way of passages. At the very end was the open commons where all the people waited, wearing celebratory ribbons. It was a trick getting Grump across from the second pillar to the third in one of the baskets, and even he was wearing a ribbon that dangled down his long nose, the end of which was billowing softly as he snored. Behind everyone there was a vast series of tables holding every kind of treat one could hope for. Candies and fruits, fizzy drinks and baked sweets, glazed yams and potatoes, and, right in the middle, a cake much taller than Yipes or Matilda.

Everyone from the stone pillars stood on either side of the pathway, waiting for Matilda to emerge. There were people four deep on either side — two hundred in all. And at the very end, before the tables of food, I stood with Marco and Yipes.

"Here she comes," chirped Murphy, who sat twitching on my shoulder. He was holding a daisy in one front paw, spinning it around and around like it was a toy.

"What did he say?" said Yipes anxiously.

"He said you look marvelous," I said. "Stop shaking."

"*You* stop shaking."

I hadn't realized it, but looking at my hand in the glow of many candles, I saw that I, too, was trembling.

"There's still time," said Yipes, looking up at me with big round eyes. "We could make a run for it."

"You should hold him by his shirt. He just might do it," said Murphy.

I pointed toward an opening in the mossy path, down the long line of people, and Yipes turned without thinking. After that his eyes didn't waver, not even for a second. Matilda walked toward him. She was dressed in a white lace dress with flowers all through her long hair. Ranger walked alongside her, obedient and quiet as I'd never seen him before. Between his teeth, he carried a wooden box — the rings — and I was struck once again by the strange collection of people Elyon chose to bring together. Two tiny people with hearts as big as thunder, a dog bearing rings, a squirrel for a best man, a boy and a girl — what nonsense! And yet I felt entirely at home, completely happy.

"Stay calm, Yipes," chirped Murphy. "Don't grab for the rings or trip over your own feet. Just take it slow."

No one else understood what Murphy was saying and I whispered back, "Be quiet. Let him concentrate."

She was something to look at, my Matilda. There had always been a little sadness in her — a loneliness, I suppose — but it was gone, and it was this more than anything that made me cry softly, for I knew my best friend had found a companion. He would still be my very dear friend, but they would have each other now. Things would never be the same.

The ceremony proceeded without delay, with only a few small hiccups along the way. Murphy sneezed four times in a row when Matilda was saying her vows, and Yipes had quite a time getting Ranger to let go of the box of rings. But soon Yipes and Matilda were kissing in the soft light of the third pillar, and the young night went from tranquil to exuberant. Flowers were thrown and food was eaten, followed by music and dancing and, best of all, skimming on the vines overhead.

Yipes had made a gift for Murphy — a tiny slider. There is nothing quite so funny as seeing a squirrel fly through the air, holding on to two knots and laughing out loud as it zooms down a long vine. I skimmed with Marco — back and forth over and over again — until my hands and shoulders ached. We walked together back to the village and the tables of food, and we talked about the next long journey we would soon take.

After a time, everyone gathered at the cake and Matilda threw the bouquet. It was heading right for Jonezy, but Ranger leaped into the air and caught it. When Ranger returned it to Matilda, she flung it low and fast and I couldn't jump out of the way. I caught it, dropped it, then picked it up again.

"Maybe you'll settle down one day after all," said Marco.

"Don't count on it," I said, but something had stirred in me that made me wonder if he was right. We were young and free and we had important work to do, but somehow I could imagine the two of us old and gray, landing *Stargazer* in the Sly Field and walking together into the Tenth City.

"Come on, Alexa!" chirped Murphy. "You've got to try the landing at the top. It's FAST!"

The fur on Murphy's tail was puffed up so that it looked two times its normal size, and his eyes appeared to be glued wide open. He was also grinning from ear to ear.

"I thought we were going to do that one together!" I protested. "You cheated."

Murphy sneezed twice and wiped his nose on his paw. "Cake!"

Murphy made a beeline in the direction of the food.

"Are you ready for the highest platform?" asked Marco. It was really high and fast.

"Yes!" came a resounding cry from behind me. It was Yipes and Matilda, holding up their sliders and waiting for us to join them. Murphy came bounding back, his face covered in whipped cream, and Ranger was close behind him.

The six of us laughed and chattered all the way up the inside of the third stone pillar. Soon I was flying faster than I'd ever flown before, with lanterns bobbing all along the way and Murphy crying *"Faster! Faster!"* from where he sat on my shoulder.

There would be times in the years to come when he would accompany me back and forth between the two worlds I'd come to know. Other times, Yipes would venture out over the water, and even Matilda came along once. There were loads of clothes and seeds and jars of honey and other such things cramping our space, and children of every age moving between the pillars and The Land of Elyon. And always, always, there was Marco at the pedals, helping guide the way across the Lonely Sea.

I have yet to venture off the course that was set for me by Sir Alistair Wakefield, but I see certain things on the old maps that make me curious. Are there other places to explore, somewhere in the immeasurable reaches of the Lonely Sea? Maybe my own children or their children will find these strange spots on the map. My way is set as in stone, and I don't feel the need to veer off any longer. It has taken many days of searching and fighting, but in the end I have found what I was looking for.

I have found my way home.